teen's
guides

LIVING
with
CANCER

Also in the
Teen's Guides series

Living with Anxiety Disorders
Living with Asthma
Living with Depression
Living with Diabetes

teen's guides

LIVING
with
CANCER

ZoAnn Dreyer, M.D.

Facts On File
An imprint of Infobase Publishing

Living with Cancer

Facts On File, Inc.
An imprint of Infobase Publishing, Inc.
132 West 31st Street
New York NY 10001

Library of Congress Cataloging-in-Publication Data

Dreyer, ZoAnn.
    Living with cancer / by ZoAnn Dreyer.
        p. cm. — (Teen's guides)
    Includes bibliographical references and index.
    ISBN-13: 978-0-8160-6484-7 (hc : alk. paper)
    ISBN-10: 0-8160-6484-9 (hc : alk. paper)
        1. Cancer in adolescence—Juvenile literature. 2. Cancer—Juvenile literature.
I. Title

RC281.C4D74 2007
616.99'400835—dc22   2007010775

Facts On File books are available at special discounts when purchased in bulk quantities for businesses, associations, institutions, or sales promotions. Please call our Special Sales Department in New York at (212) 967-8800 or (800) 322-8755.

You can find Facts On File on the World Wide Web at http://www.factsonfile.com

Text design by Annie O'Donnell
Cover design by Jooyoung An

Printed in the United States of America

Sheridan Hermitage 10 9 8 7 6 5 4 3 2 1

This book is printed on acid-free paper.

CONTENTS

What Is Cancer?

"My dad has leukemia," 15-year-old Todd said to one of his dad's doctors, "but I don't know what that really means. My mom just cries and says she doesn't want to talk about it. I know that cancer is bad, but I want to know if my dad is going to get better. I'm afraid he's going to die, but no one will tell me how bad it is."

Overwhelmed by her husband's illness and stricken by her fear of the word *cancer,* Todd's mom was ignoring her son's healthy curiosity, concern, and questions because she didn't have the emotional strength left to cope. Yet Todd desperately needed information and support to help him understand his father's illness. Fortunately, Todd's dad was being treated at a cancer center with lots of caring professionals and support groups. When one of the doctors heard about Todd's worries, he was quickly referred to one of the local cancer support groups for teens.

If someone close to you has been diagnosed with cancer—or you've been diagnosed yourself—you probably have lots of questions about what cancer is, what to expect, how it will be treated, and what the outlook may be. You also may wonder whether you'll get cancer too. Of course, nobody has a crystal ball, but you may feel better to know that most cancers are *not* inherited. Your family doctor can talk to you specifically about any genetic risks in your family (more about that in chapter 3).

Cancer is a general term for more than 100 different types of problems. Each type of cancer has a special kind of treatment, unique problems, and general outlook. Some types of cancer, such as basal cell or squamous cell skin cancers, are very common and highly treatable. Other types of cancer, such as lung or pancreatic cancer, are more difficult to treat.

No matter what kind of cancer it is, all types begin in the body's cells. Normally, millions of cells grow and divide in a very orderly way, replacing dying cells or repairing damage to the body. In a healthy person, cells are produced only when the body needs them, and then they die, but occasionally, things go awry. Sometimes, instead of developing normally, cells start dividing at a much faster rate in an uncontrolled way. Many of these cells clump together and form a mass of tissue called a *tumor,* which can be benign (noncancerous) or malignant (cancerous). If the tumor is malignant, it can destroy neighboring normal cells as it grows and damage the body's healthy tissues.

Doctors can tell whether a tumor is benign or malignant by checking a small number of cells under a microscope. (Some types of cancer, such as leukemia, don't form tumors. Instead, these cancer cells enter the blood and blood-forming organs and circulate through other tissues.)

If the out-of-control cells are malignant, they will invade and damage nearby tissues and organs. As time goes on, tiny cancer cells can break away from the main malignant tumor and enter the bloodstream or the lymphatic system, spreading to distant sites. That is how cancer cells spread from the original tumor to form new tumors in other parts of the body. This way of spreading the cancer is called *metastasis.*

Some tumors secrete substances that interfere with the body's normal functions. As tumors grow, they develop networks of blood vessels and can rob the body of essential nutrients.

Cancer can affect any part of the body, but the four most common types of cancers in the United States are lung, colon/rectum, breast, and prostate. These cancers account for more than half of all cancer cases in the United States each year. Cancers are classified according to the kind of cells from which they develop. Most are called *carcinomas,* which originate from the cells that form the top layer of the skin and some internal organs. *Leukemias* affect the blood and blood-forming organs such as bone marrow, the lymphatic system, and the spleen. *Lymphomas* affect the immune system. Any cancer that originates in muscle cells or connective tissues is called a *sarcoma.*

Cancer is largely a disease of older adults, although children can get a few types of cancer, including leukemia (cancer of the blood), bone cancer, and brain tumors. So why does one person get cancer and another one doesn't? That can sometimes be hard to understand. Jim was devastated when his mother was diagnosed with lung cancer,

Cancer Risk Factors

The most common risk factors for cancer include:

➤ age (the older you are, the higher the risk)

➤ smoking

➤ exposure to sunlight

➤ exposure to certain chemicals

➤ some viruses and bacteria

➤ exposure to some hormones

➤ family history of cancer

➤ alcohol abuse

➤ poor diet

➤ lack of physical activity

➤ obesity

because she had never smoked a day in her life. Yet old Mr. Bridges who lived across the street had been smoking three packs a day for the past 45 years, and he was just fine. This can be confusing, but research does show that certain *risk factors* increase the chance that a person will develop cancer.

STATISTICS: WHAT DO THEY REALLY MEAN?

There's no doubt about it—*cancer* is a scary word, but it's not nearly as scary as it used to be. Today, people who have been diagnosed with the disease are living longer than ever before. In fact, since the 1950s, the overall survival rate has more than doubled! And month by month, scientists are discovering better ways to treat cancer.

You'll probably hear a lot of cancer statistics and numbers thrown around by doctors, on TV, and in newspapers or magazines. How useful those statistics are depends on how carefully they're interpreted and used. For example, you may have read that the lifetime risk that a woman will develop breast cancer is one in eight—a frightening thought for women who misinterpret that statistic to mean that at any time, they have a one in eight chance of having breast cancer. The actual chance of developing breast cancer changes throughout a woman's life, so that a 20-year-old woman has a current risk of only 1 in 2,500 of developing the disease within the next 10 years, and a 50-year-old woman has a current risk of about 1 in 39.

Cancer statistics are most useful in giving people a broad perspective. They are much less helpful in trying to determine an individual person's risk, because cancer risk is influenced by heredity, race, reproductive history, gender, and personal habits.

Incidence. This term refers to the number of new cases of cancer that occur in a specific group of people within a year. For example, the total 2001 incidence of testicular cancer was about 7,200 men. *Incidence rate* is the number of new cases in a population in a given year, not counting the preexisting cases. The incidence usually is expressed in terms of the number of cases per 100,000 people. For example, the incidence rate for all cancers among African Americans from 1973 to 2002 was 505.2 per 100,000, averaging about 175,093 cases each year.

Prevalence. This term refers to how widespread cancer is in a certain group of people. For large groups of people, prevalence is estimated by collecting information from a smaller group of people and then extrapolating that information. *Prevalence rate* of cancer is the proportion of people in a population who have cancer.

For example, scientists have estimated that the prevalence of the BRCA-1 gene in the total population is between 0.04 percent and 0.2 percent, meaning that much less than 1 percent of the total population has this breast cancer–susceptibility gene.

Cancer Myths

Cancer isn't contagious, which means you can't "catch" it from anyone else. It's also not caused by a bump or a bruise, or by having a certain kind of personality.

Mortality rate. This term tells us the number of people in a group who die of cancer within a set period of time (usually a year). A cancer mortality rate usually is expressed in terms of deaths per 100,000 people. For example, the mortality rate for stomach cancer in the United States in 1930 was 28 (28 deaths per 100,000 people); this dropped to four by 1992, meaning that only four Americans out of every 100,000 died of stomach cancer in 1992.

DIAGNOSIS: FINDING OUT IF IT'S CANCER

Most of the time, someone with unusual symptoms goes to a doctor who may then suspect cancer. Often, cancer causes unusual bleeding, weight loss, swollen glands, fever, pain, or fatigue. Of course, these kinds of symptoms are pretty vague and could be caused by a number of other diseases. This is why medical tests are usually needed to find out if it's cancer. Other times, there aren't any symptoms at all, but a screening test or a test for some other reason may reveal the cancer.

Some of the first kinds of tests a doctor orders include X-rays and blood tests. If these seem suspicious, the doctor will probably refer the patient to an oncologist. The oncologist then may order other tests to pinpoint if the problem is cancer or not, and if it is, whether it has spread to other parts of the body.

A common test that many oncologists may perform is a biopsy, which involves removing a bit of tissue or fluid from the part of the body where cancer is suspected. Scientists study the tissue under a microscope to see if there are any abnormal cells.

If the tests come back positive—meaning the doctor has found cancerous cells—then the sooner treatment begins, the better the person's chances for a full recovery.

In order to plan the best treatment, the doctor needs to know the extent (or "stage") of a person's cancer. For most cancers, the stage is based on the size of the tumor and whether it has spread to the lymph nodes or another part of the body. To find this out, the doctor may order X-rays, lab tests, or other procedures.

TREATMENT OVERVIEW

Cancer treatment is aimed at removing and/or killing cancer cells. The type of treatment a person has depends on the type of cancer and whether it has spread, the person's age and general health, the person's medical history, and whether the cancer was just diagnosed or has recurred, but treatment usually involves some combination of *surgery, chemotherapy,* and *radiation treatment.* Sometimes, a doctor may recommend *hormone therapy* (treatment that adds or blocks hormones) or *biological therapy* (treatment to boost the immune system). In addition, *stem cell transplantation* may be recommended to replace immature blood-forming cells that were destroyed by cancer treatment. The stem cells are given to the person after treatment to help the bone marrow recover and continue producing healthy blood cells. Some types of cancer respond best to one type of treatment, while others may require a combination of treatments.

Usually, when someone is diagnosed with cancer, a doctor who specializes in cancer (called a *clinical oncologist*) takes charge of the person's care. Within the field of clinical oncology there are three primary disciplines: medical oncology, surgical oncology, and radiation oncology. *Medical oncologists* specialize in treating cancer with chemotherapy. *Surgical oncologists* specialize in the surgical end of cancer treatment; this is the expert who will handle biopsy, staging, and surgical removal of tumors. *Radiation oncologists* specialize in treating cancer with radiation.

In addition to these three primary disciplines, *pediatric oncologists* are a fourth distinct specialty within the field of oncology. Pediatric oncologists specialize in the treatment of children with cancer and handle surgery, chemotherapy, and radiation in the care of their young patients.

There are lots of other specialists who might help with caring for a cancer patient. A *patient educator* does just what the name implies: He or she helps educate the patient and the family about the disease. A *dietician* can help give advice on the right kinds of foods, or any special diet, that the patient may require. A *physical therapist* teaches exercises and physical activities that help a patient become stronger or recover from surgery. The *radiologist* may be called in to view and discuss X-rays or other images. Many hospitals also have a *social worker* who can talk to patients and their families about any emotional or physical problems, and who can help individuals find support services.

Treatment protocol. Each of these specialists may be involved to some degree in patient care. Because each of the more than 100 different types of cancer is treated differently, it can be hard to generalize about what kind of treatment any particular patient might be given.

In treating cancer, the doctor will follow a special treatment plan called a *protocol,* which is the accepted method of treating any particular type of cancer. Of course, even two people with the very same cancer who are given the very same treatment plan may not respond in the same way. That's because everyone's body is different, and so everyone responds a little differently to treatment. For example, one person getting chemotherapy may feel very sick and nauseated while another isn't bothered by nausea at all.

Surgery. Odds are, if someone has cancer, they are going to need surgery to remove the tumor. In fact, three out of every five people with cancer have surgery, which is the oldest type of treatment for cancer. During surgery, the surgeon will try to remove as much of the cancer as possible, including all the cancer cells. Often the doctor also removes healthy cells or tissue in an area all around the cancer, to make sure that all the cancer is gone. This is called "getting clear margins." After surgery, many doctors will inspect the tumor to make sure there is a good, clear margin of healthy tissue all around the tumor. If there are cancerous cells near the border of the tissue that was removed, the surgeon may go back and do further surgery to try to get every single cancerous cell.

Radiation therapy. This kind of treatment (which we'll discuss in more depth in chapter 6) uses high-energy rays to kill cancer cells or shrink a tumor, using either external or internal radiation. In *external radiation,* the radiation is produced from a large machine directed toward a part of the patient's body. Most people go to a hospital or clinic for treatment five days a week for several weeks. In *internal radiation* (also called *brachytherapy*), radioactive material is placed in seeds, needles, or thin plastic tubes that are inserted in the tissue to be treated, where they remain for several days. The patient usually is hospitalized for this procedure.

In systemic radiation, the patient swallows liquid or capsules (or has an injection) containing radioactive material that moves throughout the body. This type of radiation therapy can be used to treat cancer or control pain that has spread to the bone. Only a few types of cancer are currently treated in this way.

Chemotherapy. This treatment method uses powerful medicines to kill cancer cells. Most patients are given chemotherapy by mouth or through a vein, usually on an outpatient basis, every three or four weeks. However, some people may need to stay in the hospital during chemotherapy. The drugs affect cancer cells and other cells that divide rapidly, including blood cells, hair root cells, and cells lining the digestive tract.

Hormone therapy. Because some cancers need hormones to grow, hormone therapy can prevent these cancer cells from getting the hormones they need. This is done either by giving medicines that stop the production of certain hormones or prevent the hormones from working, or by removing organs (such as the ovaries) that make hormones.

Biological therapy. This treatment method gives the immune system a boost, helping it to fight cancer. Most types of biological chemicals are given through a vein.

Stem cell transplantation. After a patient receives high doses of chemotherapy or radiation, which destroys both cancer cells and normal blood cells in the bone marrow, they receive healthy stem cells through a flexible tube placed in a large vein. These stem cells produce new blood cells to replace those that were lost. Stem cells may be taken from the patient before the high-dose treatment, or they may be donated from another person. Patients stay in the hospital for this treatment.

SIDE EFFECTS

Because cancer treatments affect both healthy and malignant cells, side effects are common, although the specific side effects depend on the type and extent of treatment. Side effects will differ from one patient to the next, and they may even change from one treatment to the next in the same person. In any case, before treatment starts, the health care team will explain all the possible side effects and suggest ways the person can manage them. Some side effects, such as feeling nauseated, go away soon after treatment ends, while others, such as fatigue, may linger after treatment is over.

HOSPITALIZATION

Most of the time, cancer treatments can be given outside the hospital, but sometimes a patient may need to be hospitalized for treatment. In that case, you may wonder about what to expect and whether you can visit the person in the hospital. Often, kids are uncomfortable, nervous, or even scared when they have to visit a close relative in the hospital. That was the case with Sharon, who at 13 really hated to go see her grandmother in the hospital. Although she loved Grandmom, seeing her in the hospital hooked up to machines and looking so ill was deeply disturbing to her. It upset her so much she finally sat down with her parents to talk about her feelings. When her mom and dad realized how profoundly upsetting the visits were to Sharon, they told her she could stay in contact with Grandmom in other ways. Instead, Sharon called her grandmother almost every day and made get-well cards and posters that her grandmother proudly displayed in her hospital room. Sharon's parents took a laptop into the hospital, and Sharon was able to e-mail her grandmother about life at home and at school. She took lots of digital photos around the house and gardens, along with silly shots of her pets, and e-mailed them to her grandmother as well. In these ways, she was able to stay in touch and keep her grandmother cheerful without the trauma of a hospital visit.

PROGNOSIS

Once the treatment is over, most of the time you need to wait to see whether it will have worked. Sometimes doctors try one treatment after another to see which one works better. In some cases, treatment is over in six months or so; other kinds of treatment can last for years.

Patients with cancer usually want to know what their chances of recovery are and how the disease will progress. While doctors may base a prognosis on statistics, each patient is different. Each person's situation is affected by a unique situation, including age, general health, type and stage of cancer, and how effective treatment is. A prognosis may help you understand how serious the situation is, or may help guide treatment decisions, but a prognosis can't accurately predict how any individual will do.

Many people have heard of the magic "five-year survival rate" that used to be considered a "cure" for cancer. Experts used to think that if a cancer patient survived for five years, the person was cured. Today, scientists will usually use a five-year survival as a standard way of defining when cancer has been successfully treated. The five-year survival rate includes anyone living five years after a cancer diagnosis, including people who really are cured, along with those in remission and those who still have cancer and are undergoing treatment. For example, the five-year survival rate for prostate cancer is 99 percent, meaning that 99 percent of all men with prostate cancer live at least five years after diagnosis if the cancer is detected early.

Most kids want to know if they or their loved one will be "cured"— but don't be surprised if your family doctor doesn't use that word until a patient remains cancer-free for several years. After the cancer has been treated, many patients go into "remission," which means that there aren't any signs of cancer. If the cancer comes back, this is called a "recurrence." Whether a person can be cured of cancer depends on many things. It's best to talk to the doctor or nurse for the exact details in any particular case.

IF YOU HAVE QUESTIONS . . .

You may have your own questions about the diagnosis, prognosis, or treatment, which is perfectly okay. You should feel free to talk about your questions with your mom or dad, or with the doctor or nurse. You may want to know exactly what kind of treatments will be given, and whether the treatment hurts. You may want to know how long it will last and how often the treatments will be given. Many kids wonder if the treatment will change the way a person looks or feels. You also may wonder what will happen if the treatment doesn't work—what is the next step in that case? For specifics of what to expect with surgery, chemotherapy, and radiation, turn to later chapters in this book.

WHAT YOU NEED TO KNOW

- ▶ Most cancers are not inherited.
- ▶ There are more than 100 different types of cancer, each with a special kind of treatment, unique problems, and general outlook.
- ▶ Cancer occurs when cells begin to divide and grow uncontrollably.
- ▶ Most cancers are *carcinomas* (cancer that begins within the inner or outer body surface); *leukemias* affect the blood; *lymphomas* affect the immune system; *sarcomas* originate in muscle cells and connective tissues.
- ▶ Cancer risk factors include age, smoking, sunburns, chemical or hormone exposure, some viruses or bacteria, family history, alcohol abuse, poor diet, lack of physical activity, or obesity.
- ▶ Cancer is treated with surgery, chemotherapy, radiation, hormone treatments, or stem cell replacements.
- ▶ Because cancer treatments affect both healthy and malignant cells, side effects are common.

2

Causes of Cancer:
What Do We Know?

Ryan was only 13 when her mom was diagnosed with breast cancer, but now at age 17 she still remembers that scary time. She'd been afraid her mom was going to die, and she'd been too afraid to ask any questions. But what really worried her was: *Did that mean she was going to get breast cancer too?*

Like many teens, Ryan hadn't thought too much about serious diseases or dying until her mom got sick. Before that, cancer was something that happened to other people—not to her family. Now that her mom had cancer, Ryan wondered if there was something her mom did to cause the cancer.

Actually, doctors don't really know what causes most cancers, or exactly what triggers a cell to begin growing uncontrollably. There are some things that people do that put them at a greater risk of getting some kinds of cancer—things such as smoking, getting sunburns, a poor diet, being obese or not getting enough exercise, and encountering some kinds of chemicals and toxins. In fact, it seems as if just about every day there's another news story about some other kind of chemical or food that might cause or prevent cancer.

If you're healthy, right now millions of cells in your body are growing and dividing, building new tissues and replacing old cells. Most cancers result from permanent damage to the DNA contained in these cells. DNA is kind of like a blueprint that your cells use to know how to grow and divide. When DNA mutates, normal cells will either repair the mutation or simply die. With cancer, the cells don't die, but the altered DNA blueprint directs them to grow and divide in

Myth Busters

Sometimes people have the wrong idea about cancer causes.

▸ Cancer isn't caused by a bump or bruise.

▸ You can't get cancer by having casual contact with another person.

▸ City pollution doesn't cause more lung cancer than smoking.

▸ Antiperspirants or deodorants don't cause breast cancer.

▸ Exposing a tumor to air during surgery won't make it spread faster.

▸ Having a needle biopsy won't make cancer cells spread.

an uncontrollable way. This damage occurs either because of what's happening inside your body (hormones, viruses, bacteria, impaired immunity, metabolism, and nutrients within cells), or by exposure to environmental factors such as chemicals, pollutants, radiation, diet, inhaled smoke, or other toxins. In general, experts believe that environmental factors cause between 75 and 80 percent of all cancer cases in the United States.

RISK FACTORS

When experts talk about the likelihood of one person getting cancer, they often talk about "risk factors." A risk factor is something that boosts your chances of getting cancer at some point in your life. Of course, having a risk factor doesn't mean you'll definitely get cancer; it just means that the risk factor increases your chances of having a particular kind of cancer. Many people with no risk factors develop cancer, and most people who have risk factors never develop cancer. Still, some people may be more sensitive to these risk factors, and these people will develop cancer as a result. Over the years, several risk factors may work together to cause normal cells to become malignant. That's why knowing about risk factors may help you stay healthy.

Hopeful News

The risk of getting cancer and the risk of dying from cancer both have decreased since the early 1990s. Fewer than half the people diagnosed with cancer today will die of the disease. Some are cured completely, and many of the rest live very comfortably for years because of new treatments that control many types of cancer.

Risk factors for developing certain cancers include your age (the older you are, the higher your risk), tobacco use, family medical history, alcohol abuse, poor diet, lack of exercise, or exposure to *carcinogens*—substances that can cause cancer, such as excess sunlight, chemicals, pollutants, ionizing radiation, or medical procedures.

Age. The most important risk factor for cancer is growing older. Most cancers occur in people over the age of 65, but people of all ages, including children, can get cancer too. Cancer is more common in older people because the changes a cell must go through to become cancerous take a long time. These changes may be accidental, occurring as the cell is dividing. Or a carcinogen may damage the cell, and this damage is then passed on as the cancerous cell divides. The greater your age, the more time there has been for your cells to become damaged.

Heredity. If your parents or grandparents had cancer, it doesn't mean that you're destined to develop it too. Only about 5 to 10 percent of cancers are hereditary, which means that a person who inherits a faulty gene has a higher chance of developing a particular cancer than other people. If you do inherit one mutated gene, you still aren't destined to develop that type of cancer, but since you're starting out with a mutated gene, it does mean you're at a higher risk. For example, a person who inherits either of the BRCA1 and BRCA2 breast cancer genes has an 80 percent chance of developing breast cancer at some point. Those are pretty high odds, but it also means that two out of every 10 people who inherit either of these genes will not develop breast cancer.

If someone in your family has a cancer-causing gene change that raises the risk of cancer, it would typically be passed from parent to child. If a child inherited the abnormal genes, they would appear in all cells of the body. However, even if a parent has an abnormal cancer gene, in most cases it's not inevitable that a child would inherit it. For example, each child of a mom or dad with the BRCA1 or BRCA2 breast cancer gene has only a 50 percent chance of inheriting the faulty gene.

Certain types of cancer do occur more often in some families than in the rest of the population, including malignant melanoma (a type of skin cancer) and cancers of the breast, ovary, prostate, and colon. If there have been several cases of the same type of cancer in a family, this cancer may be linked to inherited gene changes that could raise the cancer risk. Usually, however, many cases of one type of cancer in a family are just coincidence.

If you think there may be a pattern of a certain type of cancer in your family, you may want to talk to a doctor who specializes in inherited cancers. Your doctor may suggest ways to try to reduce your risk and suggest exams that can detect cancer early. As you'll learn in the next chapter, when you reach age 18 you may want to ask your doctor about *genetic testing*. In general, doctors will not give a genetic test to anyone under age 18, even if your parents want the test. Once you reach 18, the decision about whether to have this test or not is completely up to you. These tests can check for certain inherited gene changes that increase the chance of developing cancer. Inheriting a gene change does not mean that you will definitely develop cancer. It means that you have an increased chance of developing the disease.

Smoking. Smoking alone causes one-third of all cancer deaths in the United States. Each year, more than 180,000 Americans die from cancer related to tobacco use. If you don't smoke, you'll never have to worry about that—and if you do smoke, the sooner you quit, the lower your risk of ever developing smoking-related cancers. Whether you use tobacco products yourself, or you regularly inhale tobacco smoke, it's a fact that smokers are more likely than nonsmokers to develop cancer of the lung, throat, voice box (larynx), esophagus, mouth, bladder, kidney, stomach, pancreas, or cervix. Smokers also are more likely to develop a type of cancer that begins in the blood cells called "acute myeloid leukemia."

Keep in mind that cigarettes, cigars, and pipes aren't the only type of tobacco product that can cause cancer. If you use smokeless tobacco (snuff or chewing tobacco) you run a higher risk of developing cancer of the mouth.

Help to Quit Smoking

If you or someone you love wants to stop smoking, contact:

▸ National Cancer Institute's Smoking Quitline
  (877) 44U-QUIT

▸ Federal government Web site: http://www.smokefree.gov

▸ Your doctor about nicotine replacement therapy, such as a patch, gum, lozenge, nasal spray, or inhaler.

Sunlight. By now you probably know that slathering on oil and baking in the sun can age your skin and cause damage that may eventually lead to skin cancer. The danger is not just from the sun, however; you run the exact same risk of damage if you use a sunlamp or a tanning booth. Skin cancer isn't just a problem for older people—no matter how young you are, exposure to the ultraviolet (UV) light of the sun can be hazardous to your skin's health. To prevent a problem, always:

▸ avoid the sun from mid-morning to late afternoon if possible.
▸ use sunscreen with a sun protection factor (SPF) of at least 15.
▸ wear clothing to protect the skin, including long-sleeved shirts and long pants, and a hat with a wide brim.
▸ wear sunglasses with lenses that absorb both UV-A and UV-B radiation.
▸ watch out for sunlight reflected by the sand, water, snow, and ice.

Ionizing radiation. This type of radiation comes from radioactive fallout, radon, and medical procedures and can cause cell damage that leads to cancer.

Nuclear power plant accidents and atomic weapons can produce *radioactive fallout,* which can raise a person's risk of leukemia and cancers of the thyroid, breast, lung, and stomach.

Radon gas is invisible and can't be smelled or tasted. Found naturally in soil, rocks, and water, in some parts of the country, radon moves from the ground into well water and into the basements of homes. If not properly vented, people exposed to radon have a higher risk of developing lung cancer. Two of the highest known indoor radon occurrences in the United States are located near Boyertown, Pennsylvania, and Clinton, New Jersey. States with the highest radon levels in private well water were Rhode Island, Florida, Maine, South Dakota, and Montana.

If you live in a part of the country that has radon, you may want to ask your parents to have your home tested for high levels of the gas with an easy-to-use home radon test. In some parts of the country, these tests are required before a house can be sold. Most hardware stores sell the test kit.

Radiation therapy and X-rays. Having a medical procedure is another common way that you might be exposed to radiation. If you've ever had an X-ray, this emits one type of very low-dose radiation as a way of taking pictures of the body's interior. Doctors use high-dose radiation from large machines or from radioactive substances as a type of "radiation therapy" to treat cancer. The risk of *getting* cancer from low-dose X-rays is extremely small. The risk from radiation therapy is slightly higher, but in both cases the potential benefit far outweighs the very tiny risk. Still, you or your parents should always make sure that the doctor or dentist can show a real need for taking X-rays.

Chemicals and toxins. A host of chemicals can cause cancer, and many of these known carcinogens are therefore regulated by the government or banned outright. These include aniline dyes, asbestos, benzene, benzidine, cadmium, coal tars, hydrocarbons, nickel, and vinyl chloride. To avoid contact, you should be careful when handling pesticides, used engine oil, paint, solvents, and other chemicals.

Viruses. Although you can't catch cancer just from casual contact, it is true that a few viruses may increase your risk of developing cancer. Instead, the virus can cause genetic changes in cells that increase the risk of malignancy.

Several infectious agents have been implicated; in fact, chronic viral infections are associated with up to one-fifth of all cancers. The primary culprit is the common wart–causing virus known as human papillomavirus (HPV). HPV infection is the main cause of cervical cancer and may be linked to cancers of the vagina, vulva, penis, and colon as well.

In addition, the hepatitis B and C viruses may lead to liver cancer many years after infection with either one.

Then there's a virus with a very big name—the human T-cell lymphotropic virus (HTLV-1), which can boost your risk of developing lymphoma and leukemia.

The human immunodeficiency virus (HIV) causes AIDS, but it also carries a higher risk of non-Hodgkin's lymphoma and Kaposi's sarcoma.

The very common Epstein-Barr virus (EBV)—a type of herpes virus that causes infectious mononucleosis—has been linked to a higher risk of Hodgkin's disease, non-Hodgkin's lymphomas, and nasopharyngeal cancer; while the human herpesvirus 8 (HHV-8) raises the risk of Kaposi's sarcoma. Finally, the bacteria known as *Helicobacter pylori*, the primary cause of stomach ulcers, can also cause stomach cancer and lymphoma.

Of course, it's important to remember that not everyone who is infected with a virus will develop cancer, because the virus only causes cancer in certain situations. Although vaccines against all of these germs aren't yet available, it is possible to avoid some of them. You can avoid the herpesvirus, hepatitis B and C, and HIV by not having unprotected sex and not sharing needles. There is a vaccine that can prevent hepatitis B infection; if you haven't already received it, have your parents ask your family doctor about this vaccine.

Sex hormones. Sex hormones are naturally occurring substances that promote the development of male and female sex characteristics. In some women, sex hormones also may increase the risk of breast and ovarian cancer. In the past, many women took additional hormones (estrogen or progesterone) in middle age to offset the unpleasant symptoms of menopause, but in 2003 a National Cancer Institute study found that women who took estrogen at least 10 years were 1.5 times more likely to develop ovarian cancer. The risk increased the longer the women had taken the hormone, so that women who had taken estrogen for 20 years or more were three times more likely to develop ovarian cancer.

A form of estrogen called diethylstilbestrol (DES) was given to some pregnant women in the United States between about 1940 and 1971. Women who took DES during pregnancy may have a slightly higher risk of developing breast cancer. Their daughters have an increased risk of developing a rare type of cancer of the cervix. The possible effects on their sons are under study.

Alcohol. An occasional glass of wine, beer, or liquor probably won't cause cancer, but more excessive use might be linked to malignancy. Studies suggest that drinking more than two alcoholic beverages a day for many years may increase the chance of developing cancers of the mouth, throat, esophagus, and larynx—and the more you drink, the higher your risk. There is a more controversial link between the use of alcohol and cancers of the liver, breast, colon and rectum. In particular, the risk for developing breast cancer rises with increased alcohol consumption.

Experts estimate that between 2 and 4 percent of all cases of cancer may be caused either directly or indirectly by alcohol. Add tobacco to the mix, and your risk is even higher. When a person drinks, the sensitive tissues of the mouth and throat are directly exposed to the alcohol, which can damage vulnerable cells. Eventually, these damaged cells may become malignant.

If you do decide to drink, drinking in moderation (no more than one drink a day for women, or two a day for men) can help lower your cancer risk. Different levels for men and women are recommended because men and women metabolize alcohol at different speeds; in addition, the higher fat content in a woman's body means that she cannot dilute the alcohol as quickly.

Diet and exercise. People who have a poor diet, who don't get enough physical activity, or who weigh too much may have a higher risk of developing any of several types of cancer.

Many studies suggest that diet can protect you from or make you more vulnerable to cancer. On the negative side: If you eat a lot of preserved or barbecued red meat, or if you don't consume enough healthy foods such as fruits, vegetables, and green tea, you could be at higher risk. On the positive side: The folic acid and antioxidants contained in fruits and vegetables may help reduce the risk of colon and breast cancers, among others.

Being overweight and lack of exercise can lead to a higher risk of cancers of the breast, endometrium, colon, esophagus, kidney, and gallbladder. For example, fat is a source of estrogen, and in cancers related to high levels of estrogen, such as breast cancer, excess weight is linked to a higher risk.

Weakened immune system. People who have problems with their immune systems are at higher risk of developing certain types of cancer. This would include people with AIDS, those who have had organ transplants and who take drugs to suppress their immune systems to prevent organ rejection, and those born with rare medical conditions that interfere with their immune system. Cancers that might affect individuals with a weakened immune system include any cancers caused by a virus, including cervical cancer. Constant cell division means that the immune cells are more likely to acquire abnormalities and develop into lymphomas; this constant cell division may occur in anyone with chronic infections or who has transplanted organs that continually trigger cell division.

HOW CARCINOGENS CAUSE CANCER

Of course, you won't develop cancer immediately after exposure to something known to cause the disease. One exposure to radon, or a couple of extra drinks or puffs on a cigarette, won't immediately put you at high risk. It typically takes quite a long time between exposure and the development of cancer, which is why it's fairly rare for most kids to be diagnosed with many types of cancer. The development of a malignancy takes many different mutations that must build up in a cell before it becomes cancerous. The fact that so many mutations must occur before cancer develops tells scientists that there are lots of built-in protections during cell growth.

Eventually, however, cells' DNA damage may build up to the point that the cell's cycle goes awry by the activation of *oncogenes* (genes that boost cell growth) that trigger unregulated cell growth, leading to the formation of tumors. Cancer also may occur by the inactivation of *tumor suppressor genes* (genes that slow down cell growth). For example, mutations of the tumor suppressor gene p53 occur in about half of human cancers.

A cancer begins when a gene's DNA is first altered, followed by the out-of-control growth of altered cells. This is followed by chromosomal changes as the cells grow out of control and begin to invade other areas of the body.

WHAT YOU NEED TO KNOW

- ▶ Most cancers result from permanent damage to the DNA contained in your cells.
- ▶ Cellular damage occurs either from a problem inside the body (hormones, viruses, bacteria, immune problems, metabolism) or by exposure to environmental factors such as chemicals, pollutants, radiation, diet, inhaled smoke, or other toxins.
- ▶ Environmental factors cause between 75 and 80 percent of all cancer cases in the United States.
- ▶ Risk factors for developing certain cancers include age, alcohol abuse, smoking, family medical history, poor diet, lack of exercise, exposure to carcinogens, and radiation therapy.
- ▶ Only about 5 to 10 percent of cancers are hereditary.
- ▶ Smoking alone causes one-third of all cancer deaths in the United States.

3

Your Genetic Blueprint: What Are Your Risks?

The Taylor family was haunted by cancer. In the early 20th century, five Taylor children were born: Jim, Jane, Jill, Jackie, and Jean. Unknown to doctors at the time, at least three and possibly four of the Taylor children had inherited a deadly breast cancer gene. By 1950, Jane had died of breast cancer at the age of 35. By the 1970s, Jill had developed breast cancer, and Jackie was diagnosed with both breast and ovarian cancer. During the 1980s, Jill and Jean died from lung cancer, and Jim died from brain cancer. By the mid-1990s, Jim's two daughters and Jackie's daughter all had developed breast cancer and tested positive for the breast cancer gene. The other four cousins in this generation did not inherit the gene.

Almost all types of cancer are caused by alterations of DNA, the genetic material that controls how cells behave. Sometimes this DNA is changed by an inherited type of gene mutation. On the other hand, a few kinds of cancer (such as lung cancer) are clearly linked to environmental damage and are almost never inherited.

WHERE DO ABNORMAL GENES COME FROM?

Abnormal genes can be inherited or they can spontaneously develop. Most genetic damage is believed to spontaneously develop as a result of environmental factors, such as exposure to chemicals, radiation, smoke and pollution, harmful dietary habits, or viruses. In addition, cell mutations may occur simply by mistake, as cells normally divide.

If the cellular mutation (whether inherited or spontaneous) affects cells that reproduce, the mutation can be inherited by future generations.

A cell's DNA may be changed by the activation of *oncogenes* (mutated genes that cause cells to grow out of control) or by disabling *tumor suppressor genes* (genes that keep cells from dividing too fast).

Oncogenes. Normally, oncogenes regulate cell growth, but when damaged, they can cause cells to become malignant, signaling cells to divide. Experts don't really understand what prompts the mutations in these oncogenes, but many factors probably contribute, such as chemicals (including tobacco smoke) and certain viruses. In addition, a rearrangement of a chromosome might activate an oncogene.

Tumor suppressor genes. The job of the tumor suppressor genes is to suppress the development of cancer by suppressing a cell's abnormal growth. Unfortunately, these helpful suppressor genes also can be damaged; when this occurs, the genes can no longer regulate the reproduction, growth, and death of cells. This allows cancer cells a free rein to divide and redivide uncontrollably, which eventually leads to cancer. Many, many genes must be mutated and huge amounts of genetic material must be rearranged before cancer can develop. It can take decades to build up enough mutations to trigger cancer, which is why tumors are most often diagnosed in older people.

TYPES OF CANCER GENES

Many kinds of cancer may be linked to problems with a number of complex genes governing cellular behavior. Best known are the breast cancer genes BRCA1 and BRCA2, which the Taylors inherited and cause about 10 percent of all breast cancers and at least some cases of ovarian cancer. Other gene mutations have been linked to colon, brain, thyroid, and pancreatic cancer, as well as some cases of melanoma and sarcoma.

It's not unusual to have a few abnormal dominant or recessive genes; in fact, every single person carries at least six to eight of them. However, abnormal recessive genes don't cause problems with cell function unless you inherit *two* identical copies. In the general population, the chance of a person having two copies of an abnormal

Cancer-Causing Genes

Some of the most common of the more than 100 oncogenes include:

APC: colorectal cancer

ATM: breast and liver cancers; leukemia; non-Hodgkin's lymphoma

BRCA1: breast, ovarian, pancreatic, and prostate cancers; melanoma

BRCA2: breast, ovarian, pancreatic, and prostate cancers; melanoma

CDH1: stomach cancer

CDK4 (P15, INK4b, MTS2): melanoma

CDKN2 (P16, INK4a, MTS1): melanoma

CHEK2: breast cancer

EXT2: chondrosarcoma

KIT: gastrointestinal stromal tumors

LKB1 (STK11): breast, colon, ovarian, pancreatic, and testicular cancers

MEN1: pancreatic, parathyroid, and pituitary cancers

MET: kidney cancer

MLH1: colon, ovarian, endometrial, and stomach cancers

MSH2: colon, ovarian, endometrial, and stomach cancers

MSH6 (GTBP): colon, endometrial, and stomach cancers

NF-1: brain cancer; sarcoma

NF-2: brain cancer

P53: brain and breast cancers; sarcoma

PMS1: colon, endometrial, ovarian, and stomach cancers

PMS2: colon, endometrial, ovarian, and stomach cancers

PTCH: brain and skin cancers in children

PTEN: breast and thyroid cancers

RB1: retinoblastoma and sarcoma

RET: thyroid cancer

SMAD4 (DPC4): colon cancer

TGFBR2: colon cancer

TSC1: brain and kidney cancers

VHL: brain and kidney cancers

WT1: Wilms' tumor

recessive gene is very small, but in children of close relatives, it's much more common.

TRACING THE CANCER PROCESS

Every cell in your body must follow rigid rules controlling how it grows, interacts with other cells, and even when it dies. Cancer occurs when a cell loses its normal control systems and grows wildly out of control. Different kinds of cancer have different symptoms depending on the type of cell and how uncontrolled its growth.

The whole cancer process usually begins with a single cell that goes through a series of distinct changes, each influenced by different sets of genes. In order to understand how this works, you need to know just a bit about how a cell functions. First of all, in the heart of each cell is your DNA—a vast chemical information database that holds the blueprint for building every protein a cell will ever need. A gene is a segment along the DNA that carries a set of instructions for producing a specific protein. There are about 25,000 genes, and every gene is made up of hundreds of thousands of chemical building blocks. The *order* of these cellular building blocks determines how proteins will be built, just the way the combination of letters determines how a word will be spelled.

A cell function is controlled by proteins. Some genes encode proteins needed for basic cell functions, and these genes stay active all the time. More typically, a cell activates just the genes it needs at the moment and suppresses the rest. The unique selection of genes that a cell uses is what makes a brain cell different from a bone cell. Healthy function depends on the constant interaction of many different proteins all acting together in just the right way.

When all the cells are humming along normally, you're probably feeling pretty healthy. However, when a gene develops a problem, it can cause a disease—anything ranging from heart disease to cancer. Just about any abnormality can occur, but the most common gene defect involves a single problem that repeats or deletes a DNA building block. Most cancers come from random mutations that develop in body cells—either as a mistake when cells are dividing or in response to injuries from environmental agents such as radiation or chemicals. Mistakes occur in DNA replication all the time, and luckily, cells can usually fix these errors. However, if the DNA repair systems fail, the mutation can be passed along to future copies of the abnormal cell.

In the case of the Taylor family, the mutation was not spontaneous but inherited. When the abnormal gene could not be fixed, it was passed on to new generations of the family. From then on, a certain percentage of family members were destined to develop breast cancer. Each child had a 50–50 chance of inheriting the faulty gene, and every child who inherited the gene had an 80 percent chance of developing breast cancer in adulthood.

TESTING FOR ABNORMAL GENES

If a genetic mutation is inherited, it will be carried in all of the person's DNA. This means that it's possible to test the blood to look for these mutations. Some genetic tests identify chromosomal changes, some check out short stretches of DNA, and some look for a gene's protein products. All genetic tests can help oncologists predict your risk for a certain type of cancer, classify cancer into subtypes, or predict your responsiveness to certain treatments. If you have cancer in your family, once you're 18 you can be tested to see if you have some of the more common oncogenes.

If the test is "negative." This means you don't carry the abnormal gene mutation for which your blood was tested. This can give you a great sense of relief and may eliminate the need for frequent checkups and tests that are routine in families with a high risk of cancer. However, this doesn't mean you'll never get cancer. It's still possible (and much more common) to develop cancer spontaneously.

If the test is "positive." If you know you've inherited an abnormal "cancer" gene, this means you're at higher risk for developing that cancer than a person without the abnormal gene. Some people want to know this, because it can relieve uncertainty and help them figure out ways to reduce the risk of the disease developing. At the very least, a positive result can highlight the need for much more frequent checkups. Some of the Taylor cousins wanted the test to figure out how to prevent breast cancer. For example, an inherited BRCA gene carries an 80 percent risk of breast cancer, so that some women choose to have a mastectomy (removal of the breast) *before* cancer has a chance to develop. Although this type of surgery is controversial, it can virtually eliminate the risk of breast cancer in that breast. Alternatively, a person who knows he or she carries the gene could choose to have more frequent mammograms or a mammogram/scan.

There are limits to genetic testing, of course. Tests look only for the more common mutations in a gene, which means that scientists may miss other disease-causing mutations, and experts believe that not all cancer-causing genes have been identified. There are also real mental health issues too. If you find out that you've inherited a very high risk of developing a type of cancer that really can't be treated effectively (such as pancreatic cancer), would you feel better or worse to have the results? To be told you have a gene for which no adequate treatment exists can be emotionally devastating.

There are other ethical questions. Gene tests reveal information not only about you but also about your relatives and future children. Would other family members want to know—or have a right to know? If so, when would you tell them?

Paying for the Test

Genetic testing can be quite expensive (sometimes in the thousands of dollars). Many health insurance plans will cover the costs of genetic testing if recommended by your doctor, but there may be real reasons why you don't want to alert your insurance company that you may be a carrier. If you want the test but can't afford to pay on your own, many comprehensive cancer centers offer free testing as part of research studies.

Confidentiality of test results is a big concern. There are a number of laws that give people some protection from genetic discrimination, according to the National Human Genome Research Institute. Forty-one states have enacted laws to protect people from genetic discrimination by insurance companies, and 32 states have laws protecting people from genetic discrimination on the job. As of 2000, federal employees are protected from genetic discrimination in the workplace. To date, however, a national law protecting *everyone* from genetic discrimination has not passed.

There are financial considerations as well. Some patients have lost jobs or promotions or even have been turned down as adoptive parents based on their gene status. Life and health insurance are a big concern—if a life insurance company knows you've inherited a cancer gene, would they want to insure you?

DO YOU WANT TO BE TESTED?

If you think you'd like to be tested and you're at least age 18, you'll first need to undergo genetic counseling. You should agree to have a genetic test only if *you* want to know the results—not because your parents, cousins, doctors, or insurance company wants you to. If the results are positive, are there methods for prevention, early detection, and treatment of this type of cancer? Do you think you can handle knowing the results if they don't turn out the way you hope?

WHAT YOU NEED TO KNOW

- ➤ Almost all types of cancer are caused by alterations of DNA, the genetic material that controls how cells behave.
- ➤ DNA damage may either be inherited or appear spontaneously.
- ➤ Spontaneous damage may be caused by a random mistake or by exposure to chemicals, radiation, smoke, pollution, poor diet, or viruses.
- ➤ DNA may be changed by activating *oncogenes* (mutated genes that trigger uncontrolled growth) or by disabling *tumor suppressor genes* (genes that keep cells from dividing too fast).
- ➤ Cancer usually begins with a single cell that goes through a series of distinct changes, each influenced by different sets of genes.
- ➤ An inherited mutation will be carried in all of the DNA, so it's possible to test the blood to look for these mutations.
- ➤ A "positive" cancer-gene test result means you have a higher risk of developing that cancer.

4

Types of Cancer
Most Common in Teens

There are many different types of cancer, but teens typically get only a few of these, including testicular cancer, brain tumors, osteosarcoma, Ewing's sarcoma, germ cell tumors, leukemia, and lymphoma (including Hodgkin's disease).

GERM CELL TUMORS

Germ cells develop into the reproductive sex organs—testicles in guys and ovaries in girls—but germ cells can travel to other areas of the body, such as the chest, abdomen, tailbone, or brain. These tumors are often diagnosed in very young children; however, at adolescence there is another peak diagnostic time reflecting many testicular tumors in teen boys. Germ cell tumors account for about 16 percent of all teen cancers in the United States, and teens are at a higher risk than older people for developing these tumors. The most common germ cell tumors that teens get are found in the testicles or ovaries, or in the chest or sacrum (an area of bone between the hips at the base of the spine).

Symptoms. The most common symptom of germ cell tumors is a tumor along the midline of the body, which may include abdominal pain or bloating. Other possible symptoms (depending on the location of the tumor) include constipation, urinary incontinence, early puberty, vaginal bleeding, late onset of menstruation, menstrual problems, excessive hair growth, weakness in legs, frequent urination, breathing problems, diabetes, hormonal abnormalities, stunted growth, and headaches or vision problems.

Treatment. The two main treatments for germ cell tumors are surgery and chemotherapy. If the tumor can't be completely removed or the surgeon worries that some cells might have been missed, radiation may also be given.

Side effects. Typical side effects common to radiation and chemotherapy may be expected.

OSTEOSARCOMA

Osteosarcoma is the most common type of bone cancer, and it's most common in adolescent guys who are having a growth spurt. It affects twice as many boys as girls and tends to appear most often in those who are taller than average. Certain medical treatments, such as radiation for other types of cancer, may sometimes cause osteosarcoma.

Symptoms. The most common symptoms of bone cancer are pain and swelling in an arm or leg; a lump may also appear. Some people notice more pain at night or when they exercise.

Osteosarcoma most often occurs in the bones around the knee, although it can appear in other bones as well. Rarely, a tumor can spread beyond the bone to nerves and blood vessels of the arm or leg or even to the lungs.

Treatment. As with most cancer, treatment for osteosarcoma usually includes chemotherapy and surgery to remove the tumor. In the rare cases where these procedures can't remove the cancer completely, a doctor may need to amputate part or all of the arm or leg to best fight the cancer. In some cases, a doctor can save the arm or leg by first removing the part of the bone with the cancer, but leaving the arm or leg and filling the missing bone in with a bone graft or special metal rod.

Losing an arm or leg can be devastating for teens who are already dealing with body changes. Counseling and physical therapy can both be helpful in this situation. Teens who have amputations are usually fitted with an artificial limb, which can help them adapt. Most teens are able to return to normal activities, even sports. The good news is that most teens with osteosarcoma do recover.

Side effects. You may experience hair loss, bleeding, infections, and heart or skin problems as a result of the chemotherapy treatment for osteosarcoma. Chemotherapy may also increase your risk of developing other cancers someday.

EWING'S SARCOMA

Another type of cancer that affects the bone is Ewing's sarcoma. It is similar to osteosarcoma in that it also affects teens and young adults and is usually located in the middle of your hip, thigh, pelvis, or upper arm, although it can appear anywhere. This type of cancer can spread to your lungs, as well as other bones or your bone marrow. This is one of the biggest problems with Ewing's sarcoma and other bone cancers. If the tumor is on the chest wall, you may have fluid around the lungs that also contains cancer cells.

About 200 kids in the United States are diagnosed each year with this disease, most often during adolescence. Guys have a slightly higher risk than girls, but this type of cancer is extremely rare in African Americans.

Symptoms. Common symptoms of Ewing's are pain, stiffness, or tenderness in the bone.

Treatment. Most teens with Ewing's sarcoma receive chemotherapy as well as surgery. Some patients will also need radiation in addition to or instead of surgery to make sure that remaining cancer cells have been destroyed. Ewing's sarcoma generally responds well to chemotherapy and radiation.

Side effects. Ewing's sarcoma and osteosarcoma share common risk factors and side effects from treatment. Chances for recovery depend upon where the tumor is located, its size, and whether it has spread, but both types of bone cancer respond well to treatment and are curable in many cases.

LEUKEMIA

Leukemia is one of the most common childhood cancers. Two types of leukemia are most likely to occur in teens: acute lymphocytic leukemia (ALL) and acute myelogenous leukemia (AML). Leukemia is a condition that occurs when large numbers of abnormal white blood cells fill the bone marrow and escape into the bloodstream. Because these blood cells are defective, they don't help protect the body against infection, and because they grow uncontrollably, they take over the bone marrow and interfere with the body's production of other important types of cells in the bloodstream, including red blood cells and platelets. As a result, a patient with leukemia experiences problems with bleeding, and low numbers of red blood cells (anemia), bone pain, and infections.

Treatment. All patients with ALL and AML are given chemotherapy. Some even require a stem cell transplant (which can include bone marrow transplants). Some patients are also given radiation. The length of treatment and types of medicine given will vary depending on the type of leukemia. The chances for a cure are very good; today, once they are treated, most patients with ALL and many patients with AML are free of the disease without recurrence.

BRAIN TUMORS

There are many different types of brain cancers, some of which are more serious than others. A brain tumor may originate in brain cells (a "primary brain tumor") or the tumor may have spread from a cancer elsewhere in the body ("secondary brain tumor"). Brain tumors aren't very common in adolescence (they make up about 10 percent of all teen cancers); when they do occur, they are usually primary brain tumors. Two of the most common types that affect kids this age are astrocytomas and ependymomas.

Astrocytomas don't usually spread outside the brain and spinal cord and rarely affect other organs. Ependymomas usually appear first in the lining of brain ventricles, which contain cerebrospinal fluid, a liquid that insulates the brain and spine.

Treatment. How this type of cancer is treated will depend on the type and location of the tumor. Sometimes the entire tumor can be surgically removed, but if the tumor grows into brain tissue it can be hard to get it all without causing brain damage. If the tumor is removed, it's usually followed by radiation and sometimes chemotherapy.

The chance of surviving a brain tumor depends on its type, location, and treatment, but there's a very good chance it can be cured if the tumor can be removed and more treatment given.

RHABDOMYOSARCOMA (RMS)

This relatively rare type of cancer usually appears in the voluntary muscles and belongs to a large group of tumors called soft tissue sarcomas. RMS can grow anywhere in your body but is most often found in the head or neck, the abdomen, or an arm or leg. It's typically diagnosed in very young kids or teens aged 15 to 19; RMS is more common in boys and occurs less often in African Americans and Asians than in Caucasians.

Symptoms. Symptoms may not appear unless the tumor is very large. They include a tumor that may or may not be painful; bleeding from the nose, vagina, rectum, or throat; tingling, numbness, and pain on movement; or a protruding eye or a drooping eyelid.

Treatment. Chemotherapy and radiation therapy are standard treatments for this type of cancer. The specific medications you will receive depend on which type of RMS you have and how far it has progressed. If your RMS has spread before it was detected, or if it recurs, you may even be treated with high-dose chemotherapy.

Many teens with RMS live long, normal lives; the prognosis depends on the type and stage of your disease.

LYMPHOMA

A cancer that develops in the lymphatic system (including the lymph nodes, thymus, spleen, adenoids, tonsils, and bone marrow) is called a lymphoma. The lymph system is responsible for fighting germs that cause infection. Most teens with lymphoma have either Hodgkin's disease (cancer of the lymph tissue) or non-Hodgkin's lymphoma (cancer of the immune system cells).

Hodgkin's disease can appear in enlarged lymph nodes in the neck, armpits, chest, or other places. Non-Hodgkin's lymphoma (NHL) is similar to leukemia, because both involve malignant lymphocytes and because many of the symptoms of these diseases are the same.

Treatment. Chemotherapy and often radiation are used to treat Hodgkin's disease. NHL is usually treated with chemotherapy alone. Most teens with Hodgkin's disease or NHL who have completed their treatment achieve a complete remission with no signs of the disease.

5 ▮▮▮

If You've Been Diagnosed

Tanya was 17 years old and a senior in high school when she was diagnosed with acute lymphoblastic leukemia (A.L.L.). She'd had no idea she was sick until she fell off her horse and went to the doctor about her injuries. While at the office, blood work proved she had leukemia. Within days, she was in another state having chemotherapy. Luckily for Tanya, A.L.L. is highly treatable, and she was able to attend her high school graduation, wearing a scarf, to be with her friends on this important day.

Cancer isn't common in teens, but the good news is that like Tanya, most teens who get cancer survive and return to their everyday lives. Of course there are many different kinds of cancer, but there are a few that teens are more likely to get than others. These include germ cell tumors (including testicular cancer), brain tumors, osteosarcoma, Ewing's sarcoma, leukemia, and lymphoma (including Hodgkin's disease).

About 8,600 children were diagnosed with cancer in 2001, and among the major types of childhood cancers, leukemias and brain and other central nervous system tumors account for more than half of all new cases. Cancer is still relatively rare in kids, with only about one or two developing the disease each year for every 10,000 children in the United States. Yet the overall survival rate for childhood cancers is high—up to

70 percent of all children with cancer will be cured. Their cancer will never return, and they will grow up to live a full and healthy life.

DEALING WITH YOUR EMOTIONS

Why me? Many teens who are diagnosed with cancer ask this question, because cancer seems like the worst thing that could happen in the world. The simple answer is that you didn't do anything: Most cancers in children and teens have no known cause.

It's natural for people who have learned they have cancer to feel anger, fear, sadness, or anxiety, and it's especially typical for teenagers because it's so unusual for anyone this age to have such a serious disease.

Teens feel upset because they are dealing with a very serious disease with sometimes painful tests and treatments. Side effects of treatments can be upsetting (such as losing your hair) at a time when appearance seems so important. Plus there are other issues as well; some teens with cancer who are treated at a children's hospital may at first feel uncomfortable about where they're being treated and are embarrassed to be stuck in with lots of little kids. Children's hospitals have proven to be the best place for cancer treatment for teens, which is more similar to treatment for younger kids than it is to that for adults. In addition, teens get different kinds of cancer than adults. Although you're not a child anymore, the best place for you to recover is in a cancer center that specializes in taking care of children's cancers.

It's certainly normal to have all kinds of uncomfortable feelings, worries, and fears—but the worst thing you can do is bottle them up inside and not talk about them. Many teens know that their parents are already frantic with worry, and so they hesitate to "burden" their parents with their own fears. You may feel that your friends are distancing themselves out of a fear of cancer or an uncertainty about what to say, and so they're going to be the last people you unburden yourself to. If you can't talk to your family and friends, you may think, who's left?

Talk about the problem. It's important to get help in sorting out your emotions, and if you don't feel comfortable doing that with friends or family, you may want to schedule an appointment to speak with a social worker, your minister, priest, or rabbi, or a mental health professional such as a psychologist or psychiatrist. That doesn't mean you're crazy or you're weak; there are few more stressful things that can happen to anybody than to be critically ill. It would be unusual if you *weren't* feeling upset.

Support groups for teen patients. Some kids also find that they enjoy meeting with a support group for teens with cancer, because no one knows what you're going through better than another patient. And if they're your age, that makes it even easier to connect. You can exchange information and ideas and learn how others your own age have managed to cope. There are also many medical organizations devoted to cancer support, and some have Web sites as well as toll-free telephone numbers to make it easy to contact them.

Support groups may be led by a psychiatrist, psychologist, or social worker, or by cancer survivors themselves. Many groups are free, but some charge a fee. (Some health insurance policies will cover the cost.) At a support group, you can expect to find other kids your age coping with cancer. Participants may be able to share what helped them cope or offer tips on how to handle various situations.

Many hospitals and organizations offer support groups for family members or friends of people with cancer. The National Cancer Institute offers a fact sheet listing many cancer-concerned organizations that can provide information about support groups. This fact sheet is available on the Internet at http://www.cancer.gov/cancertopics/factsheet/support/organizations, or you can order one from the Cancer Information Service ([800] 422-6237). Some of these organizations provide information on their Web sites about contacting support groups.

Anyone who works with cancer patients—doctors, nurses, or social workers—also may have information about local support groups, or you can find notices about support groups in your local newspaper or Yellow Pages. You also can find a list of organizations that offer cancer teen support groups in Appendix 1.

COPING WITH SIDE EFFECTS

Your appearance is really important when you are a teenager, and there's nothing wrong with that. It's also perfectly normal to be worried about whether your friends and classmates think you look weird. The most common side effects of chemotherapy are nausea and vomiting, hair loss, and tiredness.

Other common side effects include an increased chance of bleeding, getting an infection, or anemia (a low red blood count). Kids with cancer may lose their hair, get thin, or become very pale because of their chemotherapy.

Nausea and vomiting. Luckily, with modern medicines, these days very few kids really suffer with nausea and vomiting. It's important to take your antinausea medicine exactly the way the doctor prescribes it, because it's much easier to prevent nausea than to treat it once it occurs.

Fatigue. Many types of cancer and cancer treatments can make you feel really tired. Again, new medicines may be able to help you feel more energetic.

Hair loss. Hair cells—like cancer cells—grow and divide fast, which is why chemotherapy affects them. As the medicine kills your cancer cells, it's also killing your hair cells, which is why you may find hair on your pillow in the morning, starting about two weeks after chemo starts.

Many kinds of chemotherapy used to treat childhood cancers will make you lose your hair, and at first, the thought of going around with no hair can be pretty upsetting. You may want to get a wig or wear hats or head wraps, but after a while most teens who have lost their hair stop worrying about being bald. Once they realize that their friends can deal with it and will still treat them the same, hair loss becomes less of a problem.

You may want to talk to your friends about the fact that you're going to be losing your hair, and then you may want to talk about what it's like being bald. Your friends will probably not want to bring it up first. Some kids find that joking around about it helps everyone feel more at ease.

Sometimes, friends and family shave their heads when you start losing your hair as a way of showing support. If you're not the only bald person in the room, that can make everything a lot easier!

After the initial shock, some kids like to experiment with new looks. Try visiting the Web site of the Look Good . . . Feel Better organization, called "2beMe" (http://www.2Bme.org). Or you can call them at (800) 395-LOOK. At this Web site, you'll find an interactive style finder that will help you choose the right hat, scarf, or other headwear. In the "Head Way" section, you'll find all kinds of information about scarves, wigs, and headwear.

If you think you'd like to try a wig, it's a good idea to start looking *before* you really need one. It can be psychologically upsetting at first, once your hair does finally fall out, and you might want to have a wig all ready to go at that point. Think about what you might want to wear on your head and go wig shopping with friends. Find your own unique style.

Wigs come in all styles, colors, and types. You can go for a synthetic (they're the least expensive), a combination of real and synthetic with a "natural part" (this allows your scalp to show through, making the wig look more natural), or a totally real hair wig (the most expensive). Many experts think that a combination of real and synthetic hair is the best choice, because it's less expensive, looks great, and can be easier to style and take care of. You can actually wash and style wigs too, to keep them looking good.

Even semisynthetic wigs can be pricey, and although some insurance policies will cover them, many do not. If your family doesn't have lots of extra money, you may consider a local organization that can help you out. Many American Cancer Society local groups can help with wigs or grants to buy a wig.

There are all kinds of wig Web sites (try googling some!), and your cancer center will also be able to provide you with a list of local salons that cater to cancer patients who need wigs.

Another option is to forego a wig and get lots of funky hats and scarves. Try your favorite store, but also check out specialty shops via catalogs or online shops that make some products especially for people with cancer. Especially helpful are the turbans that can cover your head at night while you sleep.

You may find it makes you feel better to cut your hair short before it falls out. Some kids even shave their heads. Not only does this save you from finding hair on your pillow but it will also psychologically prepare you—you'll feel as if you're in charge. Other kids would never want to part with a single strand before it falls out on its own—and that's okay too.

While not all types of chemotherapy causes hair loss, typically about two weeks after treatment begins, you'll start to find hairs on your pillow or on a sofa or chair where you've laid your head. When you brush or comb your hair, you may notice a few extra loose strands. In the shower, you might feel your hair becoming a little thinner or see hair on the shower floor.

If you'd like some extra help with wigs or your appearance, you can check out a Look Good . . . Feel Better for Teens "patient session" at your local hospital or cancer center. These sessions last one hour and are coed and "parent free"—you can feel comfortable discussing relationships, appearance, hair loss, makeup, diet, and more. At the sessions, you get to experiment with skin-care products, hats and other types of headwear, and wigs with guidance from trained makeup artists and cosmetologists.

But remember, it's not permanent! About six weeks after your last chemo, your hair will start to grow back—and don't be surprised if it's really curly and a different color than your old hair.

DEALING WITH YOUR FAMILY

It's really rough on you to have to cope with having a serious disease, but it's just as hard on every member of your family. You may feel as if you have to try somehow to protect your parents—many teens feel this way. These kids worry so much about upsetting their parents that they don't tell them how they really feel. Of course, this just makes your own situation that much harder: You're having to cope with cancer yourself while also trying to take on the burden of your parents' worry. Try to remember that it's your parents' job to worry about you—it goes with the territory of being a parent.

As you and your parents get used to your treatments and get to know the hospital routine, things should start to get a bit easier. If you need any help at all in dealing with your parents, talk about the situation with your doctor, your nurse, your social worker, or your mental health specialist, if you have one. They're trained to help.

DEALING WITH YOUR FRIENDS

You can bet that your friends are really worried about you, but they probably also don't have a clue as to how to talk to you or how to handle the situation. They don't want to say the wrong thing, and so many times friends don't say anything at all. Sometimes they'll stay away, only because they feel so overwhelmed and so terrified that they might say or do something that will make you feel worse. Some even worry that they can "catch" your cancer. You may have to be the one to break the ice.

When you've got cancer, you'll need your friends more than ever. You need all the support you can get—and who can support you better than the people who know you best! Ask your nurse about whether your friends can visit you when you're in the hospital. Most hospitals will allow friends to visit if they're healthy (no colds or flu!). In between visiting hours, you can stay in touch with your friends via e-mail or any of the popular communication sites such as Facebook or MySpace.com. Most children's hospitals have some type of "teen center" stocked with computers that you can use.

WHAT YOU NEED TO KNOW

▶ The most typical kinds of cancer that teens get include testicular cancer, brain tumors, osteosarcoma, Ewing's sarcoma, leukemia, and lymphoma (including Hodgkin's disease and non-Hodgkin's lymphoma).

- Cancer is still relatively rare in kids, with only about one or two developing the disease each year for every 10,000 children, but treatment is now much more effective than it used to be. Most cancers in teens have no known cause.
- It's important to get help in sorting out your emotions, and if you don't feel comfortable doing that with friends or family, you may want to schedule an appointment to speak with a professional.
- Hair cells and cancer cells grow and divide fast, so chemotherapy will kill both; this means you may lose your hair during treatment.
- Testicular cancer tends to affect younger guys; it's the most common cancer in males ages 15 to 35, but it's almost always curable if it's caught and treated early.
- Osteosarcoma is most common in adolescent guys who are having a growth spurt; it may be linked to treatment for other cancers. It's highly treatable.
- Ewing's sarcoma is a lot like osteosarcoma, affecting teens with growths in the middle of your hip, thigh, pelvis, or upper arm; it also can spread elsewhere. Ewing's sarcoma generally responds well to chemotherapy and radiation.
- Two types of leukemia are most likely to occur in teens: acute lymphocytic leukemia (ALL) and acute myelogenous leukemia (AML); both are highly treatable.
- While brain tumors aren't particularly common in adolescence, two of the most common types that affect kids this age are astrocytomas and ependymomas. If they haven't grown too far into the brain, both types respond well to treatment.
- Most teens with lymphoma have either Hodgkin's disease (cancer of the lymph tissue) or non-Hodgkin's lymphoma (cancer of the immune system cells). Both are very treatable.

6

Radiation Treatment: What to Expect

Kyle's mom had surgery to remove a very small breast lump, and now she was scheduled for radiation treatment. Her lump had been so small the doctors said she didn't need chemotherapy. Still, he was worried, because "radiation" sounded like what happens when a nuclear bomb explodes. He didn't like to say anything to his mom to worry her, but privately he agonized. He'd seen pictures of nuclear blast survivors who'd developed radiation sickness, and it all seemed pretty scary. Would his mom get thin and lose her hair?

He was even more scared when his mom asked him to go along for her first treatment. He didn't want to go, but how could he say no? He was ashamed that he felt relieved when he didn't actually have to go in with his mom while she had the treatment. While he waited, a social worker stopped by to talk to him. Apparently his mom had sensed his fears and asked someone to talk to him. The social worker explained exactly what radiation was all about and how it wasn't anything like the high doses that occurred during a nuclear accident. In fact, his mom wouldn't lose her hair or really have many side effects at all, except perhaps feeling a bit fatigued. What a relief!

If you've ever been to the dentist or you've ever broken a bone, chances are you've experienced radiation—in very low doses—

when you've had an X-ray. X-rays create a picture of parts of the body doctors can't see. In much higher doses, this very same radiation is used to treat cancer by killing cells or stopping them from growing.

Many patients with cancer are treated with radiation therapy, which is also known as radiotherapy, irradiation, or X-ray therapy. Radiation therapy is one of the most common forms of cancer treatment. More than half of all people with cancer undergo some form of radiation therapy during treatment, according to the National Cancer Institute.

Many kinds of adult cancers are treated with radiation, including cancers of the breast, colon, ovary, and lung. Some types of childhood cancer also are treated with radiation therapy, including brain tumors, Wilms' tumor, and head and neck cancers. Kids typically receive only external radiation therapy, although kids and teens who have cancers of the head and neck, uterus, cervix, thyroid, and testes may be treated with internal radiation therapy.

Although the goal of radiation therapy is to destroy cancer cells, the invisible radiation beams also destroy normal cells, which is why doctors treat only one isolated part of the body. The good news is that if any normal cells are affected, they can recover from the effects of radiation more easily than can abnormal cells. Nevertheless, during radiation treatment the health care experts will monitor how much radiation the healthy tissue receives.

Because each patient's situation is different, each person's cancer treatment is unique too. Radiation therapy may be given before, during, or after chemotherapy. A doctor may choose to use radiation therapy and surgery at the same time, in a procedure known as intraoperative radiation. In other cases, radiation may be administered before surgery to kill cancer cells. Radiation before or during chemotherapy is designed to shrink the tumor so as to make chemotherapy drugs more effective. Doctors sometimes recommend that a patient complete chemotherapy and then have radiation treatment to kill any cancer cells that might remain.

If it's not possible to cure the cancer, radiation therapy can be used as part of palliative care, to shrink tumors and reduce pressure, pain, and other unpleasant symptoms. Many cancer patients discover that their quality of life improves after radiation. For this type of radiation therapy, the course of treatment is usually only two to three weeks.

TYPES OF RADIATION THERAPY

Treatments can be given either externally or internally, depending on the type of cancer being treated.

The Radiation Therapy Team

There are many different specialists who may be involved in radiation therapy:

▶ Radiation oncologist: A doctor who specializes in using radiation to treat cancer and who prescribes the type and amount of treatment.

▶ Radiation physicist: The expert who works closely with the doctor to plan treatment and who makes sure that the equipment delivers the right dose of radiation.

▶ Dosimetrist: The technician who calculates the amount of radiation to be delivered to the cancer.

▶ Radiation therapist: The expert who gets the patients into the correct position and who operates the radiation equipment.

▶ Radiation nurse: The nurse who coordinates patient care, helps educate patients and their families, and helps patients handle side effects.

External radiation. This type of radiation therapy is most commonly used to treat cancers. It's given by a special piece of equipment that aims a beam of radiation in a specific strength at cancerous tumors or an area of the body where a tumor was removed during surgery. In external radiation therapy, the patient usually goes to the hospital five days a week for several weeks and receives radiation from a big machine. Receiving small daily doses of external radiation helps protect normal cells from damage, and weekend "breaks" help the normal cells recover. This works much better than zapping the area with one huge blast of radiation.

The first radiation therapy treatment is really more of a planning session, when the patient lies on an X-ray table as a radiation therapist uses a special X-ray machine to define the treatment area. The therapist may take some X-rays or scans, and an area on the skin is marked with ink to define the exact area to be treated. These marks must not be removed because they allow the therapist to correctly position the radiation for each treatment.

At each appointment thereafter, the patient dons a hospital gown and gets into position on the treatment table. The therapist leaves the room and the patient remains quite still as a large machine delivers the radiation to the specific area. The patient can expect to be in the treatment room for about 15 to 30 minutes, but the actual radiation therapy will not take longer than five minutes. External radiation has no sound, smell, or visible rays, and it's painless. Kids undergoing radiation therapy can't have their parents with them because of the risk of radiation exposure, but many hospitals help kids feel as comfortable as possible. Some centers offer two-way communication devices so you can talk to family or friends during treatment.

Patients who receive external radiation are *not* radioactive after treatment, so no one needs to worry about getting close to the person or hugging them.

Internal radiation. Also known as brachytherapy, interstitial therapy, or implant therapy, internal radiation involves the injection or implantation of a radioactive substance into the area of the body where the cancer cells were located. Implants may be inserted directly into the tumor (this is called "interstitial radiation") in a catheter, seeds, or capsules. Implants may be inserted in special containers or applicators inside a body cavity such as the uterus (called "intra-cavitary radiation"). Sometimes, the implant may be inserted into a body passage ("intraluminal radiation") such as the esophagus. It may be inserted near or on the surface of a tumor (called "surface brachytherapy"), or in the area where a tumor was removed. In some cases, a patient may swallow a radioactive material. Internal radiation also may be given by "unsealed internal radiation therapy," in which a radioactive substance is injected into the bloodstream or body cavity.

For implant radiation, a patient stays in the hospital for several days while the implants remain in place; they are removed before the patient goes home. Internal radiation therapy is typically used for cancers of the head and neck, breast, uterus, thyroid, cervix, and prostate. Sometimes, both internal and external radiation therapy may be prescribed.

Patients having internal radiation usually are admitted to the hospital for several days. The radiation may be placed in small tubes implanted into the place where the tumor was, or it may need to be swallowed or injected. This can involve a minor surgical procedure.

Patients who have internal radiation therapy may be restricted to some degree in contact with others for a while, because the implant may emit radiation outside the body. Visitors will need to be protected from exposure and won't be able to spend long periods of time with the patient.

Implants may be removed after a short time or left in place permanently. Low dose–rate temporary implants are left in place for several days; high dose–rate implants are removed after a few minutes. If they are to be left in place, the radioactive substance used will lose radiation quickly and become nonradioactive. A general anesthetic isn't usually necessary when a temporary implant is removed, which is done right in the patient's hospital room.

In some cases, the implant is permanent. In this case, the patient may need to be quarantined in the hospital for a few days while the radiation is most active. The implant gradually becomes less radioactive until the patient is discharged.

Intraoperative radiation. This type of treatment combines surgery and radiation therapy. After as much of the tumor is removed as possible, while a patient is still in surgery, a large dose of radiation is given directly to the tumor site and the neighboring areas where cancer cells might have spread. Sometimes a combination of intraoperative and external radiation therapy is prescribed as a way of focusing a larger amount of radiation on the cancer cells than would be possible with external radiation alone.

Visiting a Person Having Internal Radiation

Because patients with radiation implants may be radioactive for a short time, pregnant women or children under age 18 should not visit in the hospital. Hospital visitors should sit at least six feet away from the patient's bed and follow the doctor's visitation time limits (from 30 minutes to several hours a day). In some hospitals a rolling lead shield is erected between the patient and visitors.

Hyperfractionated radiation. Some types of cancer today are treated with a smaller dose of radiation given several times a day; this is called hyperfractionated radiation. Treatments are usually separated by four to six hours. Early results of studies of this type of radiation with some kinds of tumors suggest that it may lessen long-term side effects. For this reason, hyperfractionated therapy is becoming more common in the treatment of some types of cancer.

SIDE EFFECTS OF RADIATION THERAPY

The main purpose of radiation is to destroy cancer cells, but it can also damage healthy cells, which can cause side effects. Side effects depend on the dose and type of radiation and the part of the body where the radiation was received. Some patients have no side effects at all, but for those who do, most effects are mild and go away in time. Most uncomfortable feelings can be controlled. Fortunately, radiation treatment doesn't usually hurt.

Internal radiation side effects. The area that has been treated with an implant may be sore or sensitive, so any activity that irritates the treatment area should be stopped until healing takes place.

Fatigue. The most common side effect of radiation during and after treatment is fatigue, which typically begins within a few weeks after treatment starts and can last up to six weeks after it's over. Experts aren't sure exactly what causes this fatigue, which may be the result of the cancer itself or to treatment, or to lowered blood counts, lack of sleep, pain, and poor appetite. It can be tiring to have to go into the treatment center each day for radiation therapy, and mentally stressful as well.

Skin irritation. Skin damage to the part of the body being irradiated is a very common side effect of radiation treatment. The skin in the treatment area may look red and itchy and be easily irritated in the weeks or months during and after treatment. The skin may swell or droop, and the texture may change.

Some kinds of radiation can trigger a "moist reaction" in skin folds, which can become quite sore. The health-care team can provide suggestions on caring for this problem and preventing the area from becoming infected.

Skin irritation usually fades away within three weeks after treatment ends, although the skin may be more sensitive to sun exposure for months afterward. There may also be some permanent skin color changes.

Hair loss. Radiation therapy to the head and neck may cause hair thinning or hair loss shortly after treatment begins, but radiation anywhere else on the body will *not* result in hair loss. Hair loss is usually temporary.

Sore mouth and throat. Radiation to the head, neck, and throat may make the tissues of the mouth and throat sore and sensitive and may increase the risk of tooth decay. These side effects usually occur during the second or third week after treatment begins and disappear within a month or two after treatment is over. If the throat is irradiated, swallowing and eating can be quite painful. Radiation to this area also may interfere with or eliminate the ability to taste and may cause earaches and an aching jaw. In addition, treatment may cause a dry mouth, because radiation interferes with the production of saliva.

People who wear dentures may have to take them out. Often, dentures no longer fit well after radiation therapy to the head and neck, because this type of treatment may cause gum swelling. If this happens, the doctor will ask the patient to stop wearing dentures until radiation therapy is over rather than risk the development of gum sores that could become infected.

Gastrointestinal problems. If radiation is given to the pelvis or abdomen, the patient may experience appetite loss, nausea, and vomiting right after treatment. Diarrhea may begin in the third or fourth week of radiation therapy to the abdomen or pelvis. Sometimes, radiation to the head and neck also may cause nausea and vomiting. Often patients who have radiation to this area will lose several pounds a week.

Blood changes. Radiation may result in low levels of red blood cells and platelets and in the infection-fighting white blood cells.

Chest problems. Radiation to the chest area for the treatment of lung cancer may make it difficult or painful to swallow. Patients may develop a fever or a cough that produces mucus of a different amount and color. Shortness of breath is common.

Breast problems. In addition to more general symptoms such as fatigue and skin irritation, radiation for breast cancer may cause shoulder stiffness, breast or nipple soreness, and swelling from fluid buildup in the treated area. Some women notice increased skin sensitivity and others experience less feeling. The skin and the fatty tissue of the breast may feel thicker and firmer, and the breast may become larger (because of fluid buildup) or smaller (because of scar tissue). Many women have little or no change in size.

Bladder irritation. Radiation to the pelvis may cause bladder irritation, leading to burning or frequent urination.

Reproductive organ discomfort. Radiation therapy to the pelvic area may stop menstruation or may cause vaginal itching, burning, and dryness. The effects of radiation therapy on sexual and reproductive organs depends on which are being irradiated. Some of the more common side effects are only temporary, but others may be long-term or permanent. Radiation therapy to the pelvic area in men can reduce both the number of sperm and their effectiveness, although conception could still occur.

Long-term side effects. When radiation to the head or neck is given to kids or teenagers, some experience long-term side effects that can appear months or years later and are usually permanent. Depending on the dose, the location of treatment, and the age of the child, long-term effects can include problems with bone growth, fertility, skin changes, and new tumors.

HANDLING SIDE EFFECTS

Knowing what to expect means the patient also can prepare for side effects and take steps to feel better. There are many tips and suggestions for dealing with radiation side effects, and medications may help ease symptoms as well.

Fatigue. The patient should rest and sleep as often as possible, although typically resting or sleeping doesn't often renew a person's energy. Even though the person may still feel tired, resting will help the body recover from radiation. However, total bed rest is *not* recommended. Doctors usually urge patients to rest when necessary but also to try to stay as active as they can. Oddly enough, many patients find that mild exercise (such as walking around the block) may help ease fatigue. The patient should discuss with the health-care team how much and what kind of exercise is wise during treatment. Patients should try to sleep more at night and plan to take naps during the day if necessary. Help with chores and other duties and responsibilities can also be useful.

Nausea and vomiting. If you've ever felt sick to your stomach, you know that it's hard to work up much enthusiasm for eating. The doctor may be able to prescribe medicines or dietary changes that can ease the nausea and vomiting. These should be taken within the

Foods to Avoid

Patients who feel nauseated because of radiation to the stomach should avoid rich, greasy foods and highly spiced items. Foods with a very strong smell may also cause a problem, as can food served at a very hot temperature.

hour before treatment or when your doctor or nurse suggests, even if you don't feel sick at the time. Some patients experience less nausea if they have their treatment on an empty stomach; other patients find that eating a light meal one or two hours before treatment prevents nausea. Still others struggle less with nausea if they wait an hour or two after treatment before eating.

Patients who feel nauseated before every treatment should try eating a bland snack, such as toast or crackers and apple juice, right before. Typically, several small meals throughout the day are easier to manage than one or two large meals. Best choices include bland foods such as crackers, chicken or beef broth, rice, and Jell-O. Sipping cool liquids between meals often helps (especially bland, noncarbonated beverages, such as iced tea or Gatorade).

Appetite loss. For many reasons, patients undergoing radiation lose their appetite, but patients who eat well seem to be able to handle the side effects of treatment better. Radiation patients should still try to eat healthy foods, even if they don't feel much like eating. Medications that boost the appetite are available, and many patients find that it helps to eat whenever they're hungry, no matter what time it is. Small meals are better tolerated than large feasts, and eating with family and friends is better than eating alone. Patients who need to add calories to beef up their meals may consider adding butter to their meals or drinking milk shakes or prepared liquid supplements between meals. Adding cream sauce or melted cheese to any food can help too.

Diarrhea. Before radiation starts, patients may be able to prevent diarrhea by eating a low-fiber diet, avoiding raw fruits and vegetables,

beans, cabbage, whole grain breads and cereals, coffee and caffeinated beverages, and sweet or spicy food. A liquid diet of water, weak
tea, apple juice, clear broth, or plain gelatin as soon as diarrhea
starts can help, as can frequent small meals. The health-care team
may suggest diet changes or prescribe antidiarrhea medicine. Patients
should continue a low-fat, low-fiber diet for two weeks after finishing
radiation therapy, gradually reintroducing other foods such as rice,
bananas, applesauce, mashed potatoes, low-fat cottage cheese, and
dry toast.

Skin changes. Patients can try wearing loose-fitting, soft cotton clothes to avoid skin irritation. It's also important to protect
the delicate skin from sunlight during treatment. After treatment,
patients who have had radiation to the skin should always apply
a sunblock with a sun protection factor (SPF) of at least 15 on the
affected area.

Irritated skin should be washed gently with lukewarm water and
mild soap; the skin should not be rubbed but patted dry after bathing.
Patients should avoid scratching the skin and not use any powders,
creams, or lotions on the treated area. The patient's doctor may prescribe ointments or cream to speed healing and reduce irritation.

Hair loss. If the doctor advises that the radiation is going to trigger
hair loss, many patients find that getting a shorter haircut may make
it less traumatic when the hair loss begins. Some kids or teens who
have very long hair donate their cut hair to Locks of Love before
it falls out. Once the hair falls out, many patients wear hats, ban-
dannas, baseball caps, scarves, or wigs until the hair grows back.
Hair regrowth usually happens within three months after treatment
ends.

Mouth pain. The doctor can prescribe a mouth rinse to ease pain
and irritation. Mouth pain may be a particular problem with certain
types of food, such as spices, acidic foods, or rough items such as
raw vegetables or dry crackers. Smoking, chewing tobacco, or drinking alcohol all should be avoided, because they will irritate sensitive
mouth tissues.

Swallowing problems. If it's painful to chew and swallow, the
doctor may be able to suggest a powdered or liquid diet supplement
in many different flavors, many of which are available at drugstores
and supermarkets. A nurse, dietitian, or pharmacist can provide more
information.

Dry mouth. For a dry mouth, the doctor may prescribe artificial saliva or medication to increase saliva production. Otherwise, patients can try sipping cool drinks; water is best, although some patients prefer carbonated beverages. Sugar-free candy or gum may help, but alcoholic drinks should be avoided because they can dry out the mouth and throat.

Tooth decay. Dental health can be a particular problem as well, and patients should be careful to clean the mouth and teeth often, using only alcohol-free mouthwash. Patients should have regular dental checkups during radiation therapy to the head and neck, because this treatment can boost the risk of cavities. To guard against this, patients should brush teeth and gums at least four times a day with a nonabrasive fluoride toothpaste and floss gently between teeth daily with waxed dental floss. Patients should rinse gently and often with a salt and baking soda solution after brushing, followed by a plain water rinse.

Sore jaw. For a sore jaw, patients may find that the doctor can prescribe certain exercises to ease discomfort.

Blood changes. The doctor will monitor the patient's blood cell counts regularly and prescribe medication or transfusions if the cell count gets very low.

Breast or shoulder sensitivity. Radiation to the breast area may cause a stiff shoulder or breast sensitivity. The health-care team can provide exercises to keep the affected arm moving freely. Patients undergoing radiation for breast cancer who experience skin irritation often find it more comfortable to stop wearing a bra whenever possible or use a soft cotton bra without underwires.

Salt and Baking Soda Solution

For a mild mouth rinse, mix ½ teaspoon of salt and ½ teaspoon of baking soda in a large glass of warm water.

Bladder irritation. Radiation to the bladder can cause irritation that may be alleviated by drinking lots of fluid while avoiding caffeine and carbonated beverages. The doctor can prescribe medicine to help ease burning or frequent urination.

WHEN RADIATION TREATMENT IS OVER

Once radiation treatment has been completed, the patient's health must be checked during subsequent appointments to watch over continuing side effects or evidence of a return of the cancer.

While the entire experience of cancer diagnosis and treatment can be frightening, many people who have been treated with radiation therapy go on to live normal, healthy lives. Whether you're the patient or the family member of a patient, you shouldn't hesitate to ask a social worker, the doctor, or your parents any questions. The more you know about radiation therapy, the better.

WHAT YOU NEED TO KNOW

- Many patients with cancer are treated with radiation therapy, which is also known as radiotherapy, irradiation, or X-ray therapy.
- Both normal and abnormal cells are affected by radiation, but normal cells can usually recover after treatment ends.
- Intraoperative radiation is a combination of radiation therapy and surgery at the same time.
- Sometimes radiation is administered before surgery to kill cancer cells and make chemotherapy drugs more effective.
- Radiation is sometimes given after chemotherapy to kill any cancer cells that might remain.
- Radiation therapy for incurable cancer is used to shrink tumors and reduce pressure, pain, and other unpleasant symptoms.
- Radiation can be given either externally or internally, depending on the type of cancer being treated.
- Interstitial radiation is given via implant inserted directly into the tumor in a catheter, seed, or capsule.
- Intracavitary radiation is given via an implant inserted in special containers or applicators inside a body cavity, such as the uterus.
- Intraluminal radiation is given via an implant inserted into a body passage, such as the esophagus.
- Surface brachytherapy is given via an implant inserted near or on the surface of a tumor.

➤ Unsealed internal radiation therapy is injected into the bloodstream or body cavity.

➤ Hyperfractionated radiation is a type of treatment involving smaller doses of radiation given several times a day.

➤ The two most common side effects of radiation therapy are fatigue and skin irritation; other side effects depend on the part of the body that has been treated.

➤ Once radiation treatments are over, the patient must continue to be checked to watch for side effects or evidence of a return of the cancer.

7

Chemotherapy Treatment: What to Expect

Janet was a senior in high school when she was diagnosed with Hodgkin's disease, a fairly common cancer and one that is very treatable in young people. Taking the chemotherapy drugs that would save her life meant she would lose her hair. Always vain in the past about her long chestnut brown mane, Janet surprised her family by philosophically accepting her loss as the price she had to pay to survive. In the midst of her chemotherapy, she stood in front of the entire student body to receive her high school diploma defiantly wearing not her wig but a brightly printed headscarf.

Many kinds of cancers respond well to chemotherapy drugs, which are usually given every three or four weeks on an outpatient basis. These toxic drugs are able to control cancer by interfering with the growth or production of rapidly dividing malignant cells. There are more than 100 types of chemotherapy drugs that are given either alone or—more typically—in combinations, depending on the type of cancer, its location, what the cancer cells look like under the microscope, and how far the cells have spread.

HOW IT WORKS

Chemotherapy drugs interfere with the ability of cancer cells throughout the body to divide and reproduce. Malignant cells grow and reproduce in a rapid, haphazard way, and so most chemotherapy drugs are designed to be taken up by rapidly dividing cells. This is great for the cancer cells, but there are some perfectly normal cells in the body that also divide quickly, and so the chemotherapy affects them too. The fast-growing, normal cells most likely to be affected by chemotherapy are blood cells forming in the bone marrow and cells in the mouth, stomach, intestines, and esophagus, along with cells in the hair follicles and the reproductive system. When normal cells in these areas are affected by chemo, it produces the common side effects typical of these drugs. The good news is that healthy cells can repair the damage caused by chemotherapy, but cancer cells can't, and so the malignant cells eventually die.

Chemotherapy drugs damage cancer cells in different ways. With some types of cancer, chemotherapy is capable of destroying all the cancer cells and curing the disease. To reduce the chance of cancer returning, chemotherapy may be given after surgery or radiation therapy so that if any microscopic cancer cells remain, they will be destroyed by the chemotherapy. If the cancer can't be cured, chemotherapy may be given to shrink and control a cancer, or reduce the number of cancer cells and try to prolong a good quality of life.

KINDS OF CHEMOTHERAPY

Most patients receive their treatment as an outpatient, but sometimes a brief hospital stay is required so that the medicine's effects can be watched closely and any needed changes can be made.

Adjuvant therapy. Chemotherapy that is given after a surgeon has removed the tumor, when there is a risk that a few cancer cells may have been left behind. Adjuvant therapy tries to destroy these cancer cells.

Neoadjuvant therapy. Chemotherapy that is given before surgery to shrink a tumor and make it easier to remove. This is usually a good choice for patients whose cancer can't be easily removed.

Palliative therapy. In advanced cancer, chemotherapy is given not to cure the cancer but to shrink and control it so as to extend a patient's life.

High-dose chemotherapy. For some types of cancer that are known to recur, very high doses of chemotherapy are given after an initial dose of standard chemotherapy. Since very high doses of chemotherapy usually destroy the patient's bone marrow, the bone marrow is replaced after the chemotherapy has been given. This is done using stem cells that have been collected from the bone marrow or blood. These stem cells may be collected from the patient before the high-dose treatment, or from a donor whose cells are a good match. This type of treatment is only useful in a few types of cancer.

HOW IT'S GIVEN

Chemotherapy may be given in different ways depending on the type of cancer and the particular chemotherapy drugs used. How often and how long a patient gets chemotherapy depends on the type of cancer, the treatment goals, the particular drugs, and how the patient's body responds to treatment. Patients may get treatment every day, every week, or every month. In any case, chemotherapy is often given in cycles of treatment periods with rest periods in between, to give the body a chance to repair healthy new cells and regain strength.

Intravenous. Chemotherapy is typically given by injection into a vein, which usually takes from 30 minutes to a few hours. Treatment that only takes a few hours can be given on an outpatient basis.

Catheters/ports/pumps. In some cases, if a patient's veins aren't healthy or long-term chemotherapy is required, the medicine can be given by IV through catheters, ports, and pumps. A catheter is a thin flexible tube inserted to deliver drugs into the spinal fluid, or placed in the abdomen, pelvis, or chest, where it remains throughout treatment. Drugs can be given and blood samples can be drawn through the same catheter. In some cases, the catheter may be attached to a "port"—a small round disc placed under the skin, where it remains throughout treatment. These devices cause no pain if they are properly placed. When the medication is being given, an external or internal pump controls how fast the drug goes into a catheter or port.

Pills. Some chemotherapy drugs are given as tablets or capsules, which are absorbed into the blood and carried around the body where they can reach all the cancer cells.

Creams. Chemotherapy creams may be used for some cancers of the skin, affecting only the skin cells where the cream is applied. The cream is spread over the affected area in a thin layer and may need to be used regularly for several weeks.

SIDE EFFECTS OF CHEMOTHERAPY

Sue and Sharon were cousins who were both treated for breast cancer at the same cancer center. Both Sue and Sharon were given antinausea medicine at the same time as their chemotherapy. Sue carefully followed the doctor's advice to take another dose of antinausea medicine as soon as she got home, even if she didn't feel sick. She was happy to report that she didn't experience a single episode of nausea or vomiting during her entire treatment period. Sharon, however, ignored her doctor's advice. When she got home, she felt fine and so decided she didn't need to take her medicine. Within two hours, she began to feel terribly sick and began throwing up; although she tried to take the medicine at that point, she was unable to keep anything down. She spent the next two days feeling miserable.

As you can see from Sue and Sharon's example, chemotherapy drugs can cause a wide variety of side effects, but carefully following a doctor's warnings can really help head off problems. Of course, not every person will have all the possible side effects from chemotherapy, and the same drug may cause different effects in different people. Sometimes, the same drug will cause different side effects in the same person from one treatment to the next.

Fortunately, almost all side effects are temporary, gradually fading away once treatment is over. As we discussed above, chemotherapy drugs affect both cancerous and normal cells that typically divide quickly, such as those lining the mouth, the digestive system, the skin, the hair, and the bone marrow. That's why most side effects typical of chemotherapy drugs appear in those parts of the body: hair loss, nausea and vomiting, mouth sores, and infections.

Chemotherapy drugs are toxic and may cause permanent damage to the heart, lungs, nerves, kidneys, and reproductive or other organs. Certain types of chemotherapy may cause a second type of cancer many years later. The assumption is that the risk of secondary damage to other organs is worth it if the malignant cells are destroyed.

Before a patient starts chemotherapy, the doctor will discuss the most common side effects that may occur.

Nausea/vomiting. This is the most common side effect of most chemotherapy drugs, as Sue and Sharon discovered. Although many patients dread the nausea and vomiting that was a classic problem of chemotherapy in the past, today's powerful antinausea drugs have virtually eliminated stomach upsets. As long as patients take their medications promptly and properly, most people don't get sick or even feel nauseated at all. Patients who do experience nausea and vomiting usually begin to notice these side effects from a few minutes to several hours after chemotherapy, depending on the type of chemotherapy drugs that were given. This sickness may last for a few hours or for several days. Sometimes it may take some adjustment for doctors to figure out exactly which antinausea drugs will work best for an individual.

Fatigue. This is the most common side effect of chemotherapy, related to low blood cell counts, stress, depression, appetite loss, and lack of exercise. Fatigue related to chemotherapy can appear suddenly and isn't like typical tiredness; instead, it's more like a feeling of being drained to the point that sleep doesn't relieve it. The fatigue will fade away gradually once the chemotherapy has ended, but some people may not feel completely normal for at least a year after treatment.

Infections. Chemotherapy affects the bone marrow, where infection-fighting white cells are produced. This lowers the white blood cell count in the blood, making patients vulnerable to infection. For this reason, regular blood tests are usually scheduled to track the number of white cells in the blood. The risk of infection is usually greatest from seven to 14 days after chemotherapy treatment is given, although this varies depending on the type of chemotherapy.

Most infections come from bacteria normally found on the skin and mouth, intestines, and genital tract. Being around crowds or individuals with colds or other infectious illnesses when a person's white blood count is low will increase the risk of infection. Sometimes, the cause of an infection may not be known.

Bleeding. Anticancer drugs can affect the bone marrow's ability to make platelets, the blood cells that help stop bleeding by making your blood clot. If the number of platelets in the blood gets too low, it can lead to bruising and nosebleeds, or heavier bleeding from minor cuts or grazes.

Digestive problems. Some chemotherapy drugs can cause appetite loss, which can lead to weight loss during treatment. Some chemotherapy drugs can affect the lining of the digestive system, which may cause diarrhea for a few days. Patients whose diarrhea lasts for more than 24 hours or who have pain and cramps as well as diarrhea should call a doctor. In severe cases, antidiarrhea medication may be prescribed. Persistent diarrhea may require intravenous fluids to replace lost water and nutrients. Patients should not treat themselves with any over-the-counter medicines for diarrhea without checking with a doctor.

Other chemotherapy drugs, pain medications, or antinausea medications may cause constipation. This also can occur during periods of inactivity or if the patient isn't getting enough fluid or fiber in the diet. Patients who haven't had a bowel movement for more than a day should not take a laxative or stool softener without checking with the doctor. This is especially true if the patient's white blood cell count or platelets are low.

Sore mouth. Some chemotherapy drugs can cause sores in the mouth and throat (a condition called *stomatitis* or *mucositis*) or dry out these tissues, causing them to bleed. Not only are mouth sores painful, but they can become infected by the crowds of germs inhabiting the mouth and throat. Preventing oral infections is a good idea. These sores typically appear from five to 10 days after treatment starts, clearing up within three to four weeks. Chemotherapy drugs can also make the mouth and gums dry and irritated. Patients who don't eat a healthy diet or who don't brush their teeth regularly during chemotherapy are more likely to get mouth sores.

In addition to being painful, mouth sores can become infected by the many germs that live in the mouth. Every step should be taken to prevent infections, because they can be hard to fight during chemotherapy and can lead to serious problems. Chemotherapy can also alter the way food tastes, making things taste saltier, bitter, or metallic during the course of treatment.

Hair loss. Hair loss is one of the most well-known side effects of chemotherapy. Although a few drugs don't cause hair loss (or the amount of hair lost is slight), most do cause partial or complete hair loss during treatment. Some chemotherapy can damage hair and make it brittle. If this happens, the hair may break off near the scalp a week or two after the chemotherapy has started.

The amount of hair lost depends on the dose and type of drug or combination of drugs used, and the patient's reaction to the drug. Hair loss typically begins within a few weeks of the start of treatment. Some drugs also trigger loss of body hair, including eyelashes and eyebrows. If patients do lose hair as a result of chemotherapy, it will grow back once chemotherapy is finished. Often, hair grows back temporarily curly, regardless of how straight it grew originally.

Skin/nail changes. Some drugs can discolor or dry out the skin or make the skin more sensitive to sunlight during and after treatment. Nails may grow more slowly or be discolored, brittle, or flaky.

Chemotherapy creams may cause some soreness or irritation of the skin in the affected area, but they don't cause side effects in any other parts of the body.

Nerves. Some chemotherapy drugs can cause tingling, numbness, or a sensation of pins and needles known as peripheral neuropathy in the feet or hands. This feeling gradually fades away after chemotherapy ends, but in severe cases the nerves may suffer permanent damage.

Nervous system. Some drugs can trigger feelings of anxiety, restlessness, dizziness, or sleeplessness. Some patients experience headaches, concentration and memory problems, or thinking problems. Some chemotherapy drugs can cause ringing in the ears or interfere with the ability to hear high-pitched sounds.

Radiation recall. Patients who had radiation therapy before chemotherapy may experience a skin reaction called "radiation recall" during or shortly after some anticancer drugs are administered. This causes redness, blistering, or peeling in areas of the skin that had been irradiated and can last for hours or days.

Pain. Some kinds of chemotherapy cause pain. Some drugs can cause headaches or damage nerves, leading to burning, numbness, or tingling or shooting pain, most often in the fingers or toes. Other drugs can cause mouth sores, muscle pains, and stomach pains.

Kidney/bladder problems. Some anticancer drugs can irritate the bladder or cause temporary or permanent damage to the bladder or kidneys. Some anticancer drugs can turn the urine orange, red, green, or yellow; others cause a unique urine odor for 24 to 72 hours.

Flu symptoms. Some patients may experience flu-like symptoms a few hours to a few days after a chemotherapy treatment, especially if chemotherapy is combined with biological therapy (treatment to boost the body's immune system, using vaccines, growth factors, and so on). These symptoms may include aching muscles and joints, headache, fatigue, nausea, slight fever, chills, and poor appetite. An infection or the cancer itself can also cause these symptoms.

Fluid retention. Hormonal changes as a result of the chemotherapy or the cancer itself can cause fluid retention.

HANDLING SIDE EFFECTS

Great progress has been made in preventing and treating some of chemotherapy's common as well as rare serious side effects. Many new drugs and treatment methods destroy cancer more effectively while doing less harm to the body's healthy cells.

Fatigue. Although tiredness will fade away gradually once the chemotherapy has ended, some people find that they still feel tired for a year or more afterward. The doctor will check blood cell counts often during treatment. If blood tests reveal that hemoglobin is too low, the doctor may prescribe a medicine to boost the growth of red blood cells. If the red count falls too low, the patient may need a blood transfusion or a medicine called erythropoietin to boost the number of red blood cells. The extra red cells in the blood transfusion will very quickly pick up the oxygen from the lungs and take it around the body to increase energy levels.

If possible, doing at least some exercise (such as walking around the block) can help prevent fatigue.

Nausea/vomiting. The most dreaded side effect of chemotherapy is nausea and vomiting, and yet modern medications have made this problem much less common—as long as the drugs are taken exactly as prescribed. Antinausea drugs are usually given today right along with intravenous chemotherapy drugs; the next dose of the medication is typically prescribed to be taken within an hour of the end of the chemotherapy, *even if the patient does not feel nauseated.* Patients who wait to feel sick to their stomach before taking the antinausea medication usually find that it's too late; once vomiting begins, the pills can't stop it.

Although modern medications are the best way to prevent nausea and vomiting related to chemotherapy, it also helps to be sensible about food and beverages. Patients should try to eat many small, light meals, eating and drinking slowly. Fried, fatty, or spicy foods, carbonated beverages, and very hot foods should be avoided. Many patients prefer "white, cold foods" such as cold chicken breasts, ice cream, and milk shakes. Other mild beverages, such as iced tea with a little sugar, or Gatorade, are usually well tolerated. It's best to drink liquids at least an hour before or after mealtime, instead of with meals, and to drink small amounts often. After you finish a meal, rest—but don't lie flat—for at least two hours. Breathing deeply and slowly can help when you feel nauseated.

Patients should eat a light meal before a chemotherapy treatment, unless nausea has occurred during chemotherapy. In that case, patients should not eat several hours before treatment.

Infections. The best way to deal with infections during chemo-therapy is to prevent them in the first place. Patients should be very careful to treat every nick and cut and to wear thick gloves when gardening. Avoiding large crowds and sick people during those times when the immune system is vulnerable can help prevent infection.

Patients who get an infection within two weeks after a chemo-therapy treatment (when their white blood cell level is very low) may need antibiotics given directly into the bloodstream. The doctor may prescribe medicines called colony stimulating factors (CSF) that help white blood cells recover, shortening the time when the white blood count is very low.

There are many other everyday things that individuals can do to protect themselves from infection. One of the most important things is to wash hands often, especially before meals, after using the bath-room, and after touching animals. Patients should avoid touching ani-mal litter boxes and waste, birdcages, and fish tanks. Patients should be careful using scissors, needles, or knives, and avoid standing water such as in birdbaths, flower vases, or humidifiers.

Personal care is also important, so patients should maintain good mouth and dental care, avoid squeezing pimples, and take a warm (not hot) bath, shower, or sponge bath every day. An electric shaver is a better choice than a razor to prevent cuts in the skin. Any cuts or scrapes that do occur should be cleaned right away with warm water, soap, and an antiseptic. Food poisoning also poses a particular risk for people undergoing chemotherapy, so patients should avoid eating raw or rare fish, seafood, meat, or eggs, as well as deli meats and soft cheeses.

Infection can be life threatening in a patient undergoing chemo-therapy whose immune system is vulnerable. At any sign of infection, the patient should contact a doctor right away. Symptoms to watch for include:

> ‣ fever over 100°F
> ‣ shaking chills or sweating
> ‣ signs of a urinary tract or vaginal infection (urgency or pain when urinating, vaginal discharge or itching)
> ‣ severe cough or sore throat
> ‣ any redness, swelling, or tenderness
> ‣ blisters or sores on the lips or skin

Bleeding. If the platelet count is low, bleeding can be a problem. Patients who develop unexplained bleeding or bruising should be given a platelet transfusion. To prevent a potential bleeding problem, patients should check before taking any vitamins, herbal remedies, or over-the-counter medicines, because many of these products contain aspirin or another blood thinner. Patients should be careful not to cut or nick the skin, either with a toothbrush, razor, scissors, needles, knives, or tools. During chemotherapy, patients should avoid contact sports or any other activities that might cause injury.

Appetite loss. Some chemotherapy drugs can reduce the appetite, and nausea and vomiting can also interfere with a patient's interest in food. Corticosteroids can help to boost the appetite.

Diarrhea and constipation. Chemotherapy drugs that affect the lining of the digestive tract may cause diarrhea or constipation. Health-care providers should prescribe a stool softener for patients taking chemotherapy that typically causes constipation. Drinking prune juice or eating prunes also may help with constipation.

Patients troubled by diarrhea should try to eat a low-fiber diet, avoiding raw fruits and vegetables, beans, cabbage, whole-grain breads and cereals, coffee and caffeinated beverages, and sweet or spicy food. Frequent small meals and a liquid diet of water, weak tea, apple juice, clear broth, or plain gelatin as soon as diarrhea starts can help. Patients should avoid any foods or beverages with sorbitol (an alcohol sugar).

Sore mouth and throat. Cleaning the teeth gently with a soft toothbrush at least three times a day will help to keep the mouth clean. Instead of a mouthwash that contains alcohol, patients should try to use a mild or medicated mouthwash, such as a solution made with baking soda. If the mouth is very sore, gels, creams, or pastes can be used to paint over the ulcers to ease soreness.

Bland cool beverages, such as iced tea, milk shakes, chocolate or plain milk, or Gatorade have a soothing effect. Ice cream or sherbet in a mild flavor also can soothe an irritated mouth or throat. Patients should avoid carbonated beverages and acidic foods and juices, such as tomato and orange, grapefruit, and lemon. Patients should also avoid spicy or salty foods and coarse foods such as raw vegetables, granola, popcorn, and toast.

Hair loss. There is nothing that can be done to prevent hair loss caused by certain chemotherapy drugs. Although nothing can prevent the hair from falling out, some patients shave their heads ahead of time to prevent the trauma of gradual loss. A variety of hats, scarves, or wigs can cover the hair loss and boost the patient's psychological well-being. The scalp will be especially sensitive and should not be exposed to the direct sun.

Hair loss can be one of the most difficult psychological aspects to cancer treatment. It can really help if the patient can talk to someone who has already been through the experience. It's perfectly normal to feel angry or depressed, but it may help to understand that hair loss is a temporary side effect.

Patients who plan to buy a wig or hairpiece should do so before losing most of their hair, so that the wig can be matched to the person's current hair style and color. Many cancer centers have lists of local wig stores that cater to cancer patients. It's also possible to purchase a wig or hairpiece through a catalog, the Internet, or by phone. Some patients find it just as easy to borrow a wig or hairpiece. The hospital's social work department may be able to help you locate local resources for free wigs.

Wigs can be expensive—especially wigs made of real hair, or real/ synthetic blends. Some health insurance policies cover the cost of a hairpiece needed because of cancer treatment; patients should ask their doctor for a wig "prescription" for a "scalp prosthesis." In any case, it is a tax-deductible expense.

Pain. After her first chemotherapy treatment for her breast cancer, Sarah developed a severe headache an hour or so later. When she told the nurse the second time, the staff arranged to deliver the medications more slowly. This time, the headache was not quite so bad but still uncomfortable. For her third treatment, the pharmacist recommended that the drugs be diluted with water and slowed down even more; this time, she was headache free. By working together, the staff was able to figure out how to give her drugs and avoid her pain.

Patients should not assume that pain is unavoidable. Doctors and nurses can't help if they don't know that someone is experiencing pain. As Sarah did, patients should talk with the doctor, nurse, or pharmacist about any pain, using a pain scale from 0 to 10 to describe the intensity.

It's best to prevent pain rather than treat it once it occurs, as Sarah's pharmacist was able to do. If the pain can't be prevented, it can be treated. Patients with persistent or chronic pain should take pain medicine on a regular schedule, without skipping doses. Patients who wait until the pain breaks through will find it's harder to control. Relaxation exercises such as deep breathing or meditation when taking pain medicine can help reduce tension and anxiety.

There are many different medicines to control cancer pain. Patients who are in pain and who can't get relief from their doctors should

Vaccination Alert

Travelers should keep in mind that patients undergoing chemotherapy should not have any "live virus" vaccines, including polio, measles, rubella (German measles), MMR (measles, mumps, and rubella), BCG (tuberculosis), yellow fever, and typhoid medicine. Other vaccines should not cause problems to chemotherapy patients, such as diphtheria, tetanus, flu, hepatitis B, hepatitis A, rabies, cholera, and typhoid injections.

consult a pain specialist. Many cancer centers have pain centers on the premises.

Kidney/bladder problems. Patients who experience bladder or kidney irritation can drink plenty of fluids to ensure good urine flow and help prevent problems.

Fluid retention. Patients who are retaining fluid during chemotherapy may need to avoid salty foods; a diuretic may be needed to help the body get rid of excess fluids.

Radiation recall. A cool, wet compress over the affected area can ease discomfort. Soft, nonirritating fabrics and cotton underwear are good choices.

WHAT YOU NEED TO KNOW

- ▶ Chemotherapy drugs interfere with the ability of rapidly dividing cancer cells throughout the body to divide and reproduce.
- ▶ Chemotherapy also affects fast-growing normal cells of the bone marrow and mouth, stomach, intestines, esophagus, hair follicles, and the reproductive system.
- ▶ Chemotherapy drugs are usually given every three or four weeks on an outpatient basis.
- ▶ There are more than 100 types of chemotherapy drugs that are given either alone or in combinations, depending on the type

of cancer, its location, what the cancer cells look like under the microscope, and how far the cells have spread.

➤ Neoadjuvant chemotherapy is given before surgery to shrink a tumor and make it easier to remove.

➤ Adjuvant chemotherapy is given after a surgeon has removed a cancerous tumor, when there is a risk that a few cancer cells may have been left behind.

➤ Palliative chemotherapy is used in advanced cancer not as a cure but to improve quality of life.

➤ Chemotherapy may be given by injection or via a port or catheter, or as a pill or cream.

➤ Chemotherapy drugs cause a wide variety of temporary side effects, including hair loss, fatigue, infection risk, appetite loss, and mouth sores.

➤ Chemotherapy drugs may permanently damage the heart, lungs, nerves, kidneys, reproductive or other organs, or may trigger a second type of cancer many years later.

8

Preventing Cancer:
How You Can Live a Healthy Life

Not all kinds of cancer are preventable, but you'd be surprised at the number of cancers that can be prevented by making the right lifestyle choices. As scientists begin to understand different risk factors associated with cancer, it's becoming clearer that there are lots of ways to avoid getting cancer. In fact, if people made better decisions regarding diet, exercise, healthy weight, and tobacco use, the incidence of cancer around the world could be reduced by up to 70 percent.

If you never smoke, odds are you won't get lung or throat cancer. If you don't have multiple sexual partners, your risk of getting genital warts—and hence, cervical cancer—are very much lower. If you don't get sunburned, you're much less likely to get skin cancer. Getting a colonoscopy every five to 10 years after age 50 will significantly reduce the risk of colon cancer. Making sure your parents keep your house free from radon also can help reduce your lung cancer risk.

It's also clear that diet and exercise certainly help lower the risk of some types of cancer. This is especially true for teenage girls, whose amount of body fat at adolescence appears to be linked to the risk of developing breast cancer years later.

The American Cancer Society advises Americans who want to reduce the risk of cancer to:

➤ Eat a mostly plant-based diet, including five or more servings of fruits and vegetables each day

- Eat whole grains instead of processed or refined grains and sugar
- Limit consumption of high-fat foods, particularly from animal sources
- Get lots of physical activity
- Limit the consumption of alcohol

SEXUAL PRACTICES AND CANCER

Certain cancers that are related to infectious substances can be spread through sexual means. This includes viruses such as hepatitis B virus (HBV), which can cause liver cancer; human papillomavirus virus (HPV), which can cause cervical cancer; and the AIDS virus (HIV), which can lead to Kaposi's sarcoma. Vaccines can protect you against HBV and HPV, but there is no vaccine for HIV. If you're having sex, you should always use latex condoms correctly every time you have sex. Their proper use may reduce transmission of these viruses.

HPV virus. The biggest news in preventing sexually induced cancers is the HPV vaccine, a newly approved vaccine that protects against the four types of HPV most likely to cause cervical cancer. These four HPV virus types together cause 70 percent of cervical cancers and 90 percent of all genital warts.

The vaccine, called Gardasil, is given via a series of three shots over a six-month period. It's recommended for any girl 11 or 12 years old (although it can be given as early as age nine), as well as any girl or woman aged 13 through 26. The vaccine is recommended for very young girls because, ideally, the vaccine should be given before a person is sexually active: The vaccine is most effective in girls and women who haven't yet acquired any of the four HPV types covered by the vaccine. Because the vaccine has only been widely studied in girls and women aged nine to 26, it's not yet recommended for older women.

If you're already sexually active, you can still benefit from the vaccine, although you may have already acquired one or more HPV types. However, few young women are infected with all four of these critical HPV types, so you would still be protected from any types you have not acquired. At the moment, there is no test that can tell which of these four HPV types you may have. If you already have HPV, genital warts, precancer, or cancer, the vaccine won't help treat these conditions.

Researchers aren't yet sure how long protection lasts with this vaccine. At the moment, scientists know that the vaccine lasts for at least five years. Whether or not a booster may someday be necessary has not yet been determined.

What about boys? They certainly also can get these warts, but researchers don't yet know if the vaccine is effective in boys or men. It's possible that vaccinating boys could prevent them from getting genital warts and rare cancers, such as penile and anal cancer. Scientists are now studying whether the vaccine can prevent HPV infection and disease in boys. If it is effective, this vaccine may be licensed and recommended for boys and men as well.

Hepatitis B vaccine. This vaccine was the very first anticancer vaccine ever approved. It prevents hepatitis B disease and its serious consequence—liver cancer. At the moment, hep B vaccine is given to all infants at birth, and again at age one month and six months. If by adolescence you haven't yet been vaccinated for hep B, you should do so immediately. It's a series of three shots, given one month and six months after the first. "Recombivax HB" has been approved as a two-dose schedule for kids aged 11 to 15 years. Studies show that the vaccine should protect you for at least 23 years.

DIET

What kid doesn't love pizza, soda, and burgers? It's hard to imagine that what you eat now could affect how likely it is you'll develop cancer someday, but it's true. Of course, an occasional fast-food foray won't kill you. What you need to start thinking about *today*, however, is how to start adding healthier foods to your diet.

What's healthy? You probably already have a pretty good idea. Many of the most common fruits and vegetables contain cancer-fighting properties, including *antioxidants* that neutralize potential cell damage and the powerful *phytochemicals* (plant-based chemicals) that scientists are just beginning to understand.

Although experts don't understand exactly how diet is related to cancer, research has shown that the kind of food you eat does play a role in preventing cancer. For example, people in parts of the world who tend to eat at least five servings of fruits and vegetables a day have lower rates of some of the most common cancers.

Fruits and vegetables contain lots of antioxidants and phytochemicals, such as vitamins A, C, and E, and beta-carotene, which have been shown to prevent cancer. However, it's not completely clear whether it is the individual phytochemical or a combination of them, or whether it's the fiber in fruits and vegetables, that lower the risk of cancer. That's why the best thing you can do is eat a variety of fresh vegetables and fruits. Here's an A-to-Z listing of the best choices:

Avocados. These vegetables have lots of a type of antioxidant that blocks the intestinal absorption of certain fats, while supplying lots of potassium and beta-carotene.

Broccoli, brussels sprouts, cabbage, and cauliflower. Most kids aren't wild about any of these "cruciferous" vegetables, but they're terrific at preventing cancer. They all contain two antioxidants that may help decrease prostate and other cancers. They also have a chemical component that can combat breast cancer by converting a cancer-promoting estrogen into a more protective type. Broccoli and broccoli sprouts (trade name: BroccoSprouts) also have a phytochemical that some experts believe can help prevent colon and rectal cancer. The funny-sounding BroccoSprouts have as much as 20 times the cancer-fighting ingredients of mature heads of broccoli.

Carrots. Who doesn't love a carrot? These contain lots of beta-carotene, and raw carrots may help reduce a wide range of cancers including lung, mouth, throat, stomach, intestine, bladder, prostate, and breast. As in the case of carrots, some cancer-fighting substances are destroyed when cooked. So eat your carrots raw, when possible.

Chili peppers and jalapeños. If you like your Mexican food spicy, you're in luck. These peppers contain capsaicin, which may neutralize certain cancer-causing substances and may help prevent stomach cancer.

Citrus fruits. Grapefruit, oranges, and other citrus fruits help prevent cancer by sweeping carcinogens out of the body. Some studies show that grapefruit may inhibit the growth of breast-cancer cells. Oranges and lemons contain a substance that stimulates cancer-killing immune cells.

Flax. You can get flax by eating flax seeds—a substance that may have an antioxidant effect and block or suppress cancerous changes in cells. Flax is also high in omega-3 fatty acids, which experts believe may help protect against colon cancer (not to mention heart disease). Flax seeds are typically eaten in ground form; ground flax can be sprinkled on cereal, yogurt, or a variety of other foods.

Garlic, leeks, and chives. You may want to avoid these foods if you're getting ready for a date and you don't want stinky breath, but these foods seem to be powerful anticancer fighters. Garlic has immune-enhancing compounds that seem to boost the activity of cancer-fighting immune cells and that help block carcinogens from entering cells, slowing the development of tumors. A component of garlic oil also has been shown to inactivate liver carcinogens.

Other studies have linked garlic, onions, leeks, and chives to lower risk of stomach and colon cancer. According to one report, people who regularly chow down on raw or cooked garlic have about half the risk of stomach cancer and two-thirds the risk of colorectal cancer as people who avoid these foods. If you're worried about smelly breath, garlic supplements have the same effect as the real thing.

Experts suspect that garlic may help prevent stomach cancer because it fights the bacterium (*Helicobacter pylori*) that promotes stomach cancer.

Grapes (red). Red grapes contain powerful antioxidants called *bioflavonoids* that prevent cancer. Grapes also have a substance that inhibits the enzymes that can stimulate cancer-cell growth and suppress immune response. In addition, red grapes contain ellagic acid, which can help slow tumor growth by blocking enzymes necessary for cancer cells to thrive.

Kale. Not a popular green leafy vegetable, kale contains nitrogen compounds that may help stop cancerous cells from developing in estrogen-sensitive tissues. In addition, phytochemicals found in kale may suppress tumor growth and block cancer-causing substances.

Mushrooms. The mushrooms commonly found on top of your pizza may be tasty, but it's the more exotic varieties that may help prevent cancer and boost your immune system. Shiitake, maitake, reishi, *Agaricus blazei Murill,* and Coriolus Versicolor contain powerful compounds that help build immunity and attack cancerous cells and prevent them from multiplying. These mushrooms also can stimulate the production of viral-fighting interferon in the body. (Interferon is a protein produced by infected cells that seems to help the immune system and is used to help treat many cancers.) So helpful are these mushrooms that an extract has been successfully tested in recent years in Japan as an addition to chemotherapy treatment.

Nuts. These tasty snacks contain antioxidants that may suppress the growth of cancers. The Brazil nut contains selenium, which is important against prostate cancer.

Papayas. More common than they used to be on grocery shelves, papayas are a good source of vitamin C, which serves as an antioxidant and also may reduce absorption of cancer-causing substances from the soil or from processed foods. Papaya also contains folic acid, which has been shown to interfere with certain cancers.

Raspberries. These little fruits contain many vitamins, minerals, plant compounds, and antioxidants that may protect against cancer. According to a recent research study, rats that ate black raspberries had from 43 to 62 percent drop in esophageal tumors. Other research suggests that black raspberries also may guard against colon cancer. Black raspberries are rich in antioxidants and are believed to have even more cancer-preventing properties than blueberries or strawberries.

Red wine. *In moderation,* red wine appears to contain strong antioxidants that may protect against various types of cancer. And a substance in grape skins appears to help prevent cancer. It's important to remember that drinking alcohol is illegal for anyone under age 21. In addition, alcohol can be toxic to the liver and to the nervous system, and many wines have sulfites, to which many people are allergic.

Rosemary. This green herb may boost the activity of enzymes that detoxify harmful substances in your body. An extract of rosemary (carnosol) has interfered with the development of both breast and skin tumors in animals, although no studies have been done on humans. You can use rosemary as a seasoning or drink it as a tea.

Seaweed. It may not look very appetizing floating in the ocean, but seaweed packs a nutritional wallop, including beta-carotene, protein, vitamin B12, fiber, and chlorophyll. All of these substances may help fight against breast cancer. You can find seaweed extracts in pill form on health-food shelves.

Soy products. The most popular of these is tofu, which contains several types of plant-based estrogens that could help prevent both breast and prostate cancer by blocking and suppressing cancerous changes in cells. There are a number of substances in soy products that halt the growth and spread of cancerous cells. Soy products appear to lower breast-cancer risk by inhibiting the growth of certain cells and new blood vessels that tumors need to grow. So powerful is this benefit that soy is being studied as a potential anticancer drug.

This doesn't mean you should run right out and stock up on all types of soy products. Eating up to four or five ounces of soy products daily is probably safe, but some scientists worry that overloading on soy could cause hormone imbalances that stimulate cancer growth. If you're at high risk for developing breast cancer (if your mom, aunts, grandmother, or sisters have cancer, or if the breast cancer gene is in your family), you should talk to your doctor before eating a lot of soy products.

Sweet potatoes. These sweet vegetables contain many anticancer properties, including beta-carotene, which may protect your DNA from cancer-causing chemicals.

Teas. Both green and black teas contain certain antioxidants that appear to prevent cancer cells from dividing. Green tea—that's what you get in Asian restaurants—is your best choice, followed by the more common black tea.

Dry green tea leaves may reduce the risk of cancer of the stomach, lung, colon, rectum, liver, and pancreas, according to a number of studies.

Tomatoes. This popular vegetable contains lycopene, an antioxidant that attacks a type of oxygen molecule ("free radicals") suspected of triggering cancer. It appears that the hotter the weather, the more lycopene tomatoes produce. Tomatoes are also a good source of vitamin C, which can prevent cancer-causing cellular damage.

Lycopene has been shown to kill mouth cancer cells and can reduce the risk for developing breast, prostate, pancreas, and colorectal cancer.

These anticancer substances are made even more potent by cooking, and recent studies indicate that for proper absorption, the body also needs some oil along with lycopene.

Herbal Teas Don't Help

Although herbal teas may be yummy, they don't appear to help prevent cancer.

Avoid Fat to Avoid Cancer

People who eat a low-fat (especially animal fat) diet have lower cancer rates, although it isn't clear whether the cause is the fewer calories consumed, the amount and distribution of a person's body fat, or the fact that someone watching their fat intake is probably also eating fiber, fruits, and vegetables that protect against cancer.

EXERCISE

Sure, it's fun to play video games and spend time hanging out on MySpace, Facebook, Xanga, YouTube, and all those other cool Internet sites, but the more time you spend in front of the TV and the computer, the less time you spend outdoors getting healthy exercise. That really does matter when it comes to cancer, because there's strong evidence that exercise is linked to a lower risk of a variety of cancers.

Breast cancer. Exercise is especially helpful in warding off cancers of the breast. Physically active girls and women of all ages have up to a 40 percent reduced risk of developing breast cancer, and start now, because experts believe a lifetime of regular, vigorous activity is of greatest benefit in preventing breast cancer. Still, even occasional exercise is better than nothing; women who occasionally engage in physical activity also have a lower breast cancer risk.

Interestingly, the protective benefit of exercise occurs only if you're of normal weight (but, of course, if you're a bit overweight and you start exercising, you'll soon lose pounds and then you'll gain the breast cancer benefits).

Colon cancer. Exercise is also especially helpful in warding off cancers of the colon. Physically active people can cut the risk of developing colon cancer by 40 to 50 percent—and the more active you are, the higher the risk reduction.

Other cancers. In addition, several studies have reported links between exercise and a reduced risk of prostate, lung, and endometrial (lining of the uterus) cancers. Studies also suggest that women who are physically active have a 30 to 40 percent reduced risk of endometrial cancer, with the greatest reduction in risk among those who are most active. Some studies suggest that individuals who are physically active have a 30 to 40 percent reduced risk of developing lung cancer.

How does exercise prevent cancer? In part, exercise may reduce cancer risk because people who exercise tend not to be overweight— and obesity is a risk factor for many types of cancer.

In the case of breast cancer, vigorous physical activity may decrease the exposure of breast tissue to circulating estrogen, a hormone that has been implicated in breast cancer.

Colon cancer may occur less often in active individuals because physical activity speeds up the movement of food through the intestine, reducing the length of time that the bowel lining is exposed to potential carcinogens. This results in a lower risk for colon cancer.

In addition, physical activity may improve energy metabolism and reduce circulating concentrations of insulin and related growth factors that have been implicated in many types of cancer development.

How much is enough? The Centers for Disease Control and Prevention (CDC) recommend that you should engage in moderate physical activity for at least 30 minutes at least five days a week or vigorous activity for at least 20 minutes at least three days a week.

SMOKING AND CANCER

About 30 percent of all cancers are due to tobacco use, and almost all lung cancers are caused by smoking. If you want to prevent lung cancer, the advice is simple: Don't smoke. If you're already smoking, stop.

SUNBURN AND CANCER

Many skin cancers can be prevented by protection from sunlight. This doesn't mean you have to live like a mole and never show your face in daytime. It does mean you should use sunscreen and avoid tanning beds.

If you like that allover healthy glow, use a tanning product or get a spray-on tan (also called "sunless tanning"). However, tanning products and sunless tanning won't protect you from UV radiation; you can still get burned after using these products if you go out in the sun and don't use a sunscreen.

GET SCREENED!

Eating right, avoiding the sun, and exercising are all great, but it's also a good idea—especially as you get older—to get screened for certain types of cancers. Getting a cancer screening means looking for cancer before it causes any symptoms. In general, the earlier a cancer is treated, the more effective that treatment will be. In particular, screening tests are used to check for cancers of the breast, cervix, colon, and rectum.

You may want to talk with your doctor about the possible benefits of being checked for cancer. The decision to be screened, like many other medical decisions, is a personal one. Each person should decide after learning about the pros and cons of screening. Typically, teens aren't normally candidates for cancer screening because most types of these cancers only occur later in life.

Breast. A mammogram is the best tool doctors have to find breast cancer early in women of average risk. A mammogram is a picture of the breast made with X-rays.

Teens don't typically have to worry about getting a mammogram, but if you have a family history of the breast cancer genes (BRCA1 and BRCA2), you might want to consider being tested for the gene itself. If you do have the gene, experts recommend that you begin surveillance with a clinical breast exam at age 18 and have your first baseline mammogram at age 25, with annual mammograms every year thereafter. If you belong to this very high risk group of women, you should also know that research suggests that MRI (magnetic resonance imaging) is a much more effective way to detect breast cancer. Studies also found that combination screening—that is, an MRI together with a mammogram, a clinical breast exam, and an ultrasound—found 95 percent of breast cancers (compared to 36 percent by mammogram alone).

For girls and women with an average breast cancer risk, however, the benefits of MRI screening don't seem to be so dramatic. Despite its limitations, mammography is still considered the best screening method for such women. If you're only at average risk for breast cancer, the NCI recommends that women over age 40 have a mammogram once every one or two years.

Cervix. The *Pap test* (sometimes called Pap smear) is used to check cells from the cervix. In this test, a doctor scrapes a sample of cells from the cervix, and the lab checks those cells for cancer or changes that may lead to cancer (including changes caused by HPV, the most important risk factor for cancer of the cervix).

HPV Vaccine and Pap Tests

Because the HPV vaccine doesn't protect against all types of HPV, it won't prevent all cases of cervical cancer or genital warts. The vaccine won't prevent about 30 percent of cervical cancers, so it's important for you to continue to be screened for cervical cancer with a regular Pap test. Also, the vaccine can't prevent about 10 percent of genital warts, so it's still important, if you're sexually active, to reduce your exposure to HPV.

Even if you've had the HPV vaccine (Gardasil), you should start having Pap tests three years after you first start having sexual intercourse or when you reach age 21 (whichever comes first) and continue to have a Pap test at least once every three years. (Some women should have a Pap test more often; discuss frequency with your doctor.)

Colon and rectum. A number of screening tests are used to detect growths (*polyps*), cancer, or other problems in the colon and rectum—but you won't have to worry about these for a few years yet. These screening tests are typically advised for people aged 50 and older. Adults with a higher-than-average risk of cancer of the colon or rectum should talk with their doctor about whether to have screening tests before age 50 and how often to have them.

Sometimes cancer or polyps bleed, so a *fecal occult blood test* can detect tiny amounts of blood in the stool. In a test called a *sigmoidoscopy*, the doctor checks inside the rectum and lower part of the colon with a lighted tube called a *sigmoidoscope*. Any polyps can usually be removed right through the tube.

In a *colonoscopy*, the doctor examines the rectum and entire colon using a lighted tube called a *colonoscope*. Any polyps can usually be removed right through the tube.

A *double-contrast barium enema* involves taking X-rays of the colon and rectum after the patient is given an enema with a barium solution, and air is pumped into the rectum. The barium and air improve the X-ray images of the colon and rectum.

During a *digital rectal exam,* a health-care provider inserts a lubricated, gloved finger into the lowest part of the rectum to feel for abnormal areas.

WHAT YOU NEED TO KNOW

- Many types of cancer can be prevented by making the right lifestyle choices.
- Up to 70 percent of all cancer could be prevented if people stopped smoking and made better decisions regarding diet, exercise, and healthy weight.
- To lower the risk of cancer, you should eat five or more servings of fruits and vegetables each day; eat whole grains instead of processed or refined grains and sugar; limit consumption of high-fat foods, particularly from animal sources; exercise; and don't drink too much alcohol.
- About 70 percent of cervical cancers can be prevented with a new vaccine that protects against four types of human papillomavirus (HPV).
- The hepatitis B (HBV) vaccine protects against liver cancer.
- Using latex condoms correctly each time you have sex can reduce transmission of cancer-causing viruses (HIV, HPV, and HBV).
- Eating at least five servings of fruits and vegetables a day can help prevent cancer.
- Avoiding fat (especially animal fat) can help prevent cancer.
- Exercise five days a week is linked to a lower risk of a variety of cancers.
- Stopping smoking can prevent lung cancer.
- Avoiding excess exposure to the sun can prevent skin cancer.
- Screening tests can check for early cancers of the breast, cervix, colon, and rectum; teen girls should have a Pap smear within three years of having sex or by age 21, whichever comes first.

9

When Someone You Love Has Cancer

Karen and Katie were 16 and 14 when their mom was diagnosed with breast cancer. They were scared about their mom, worrying about whether she was going to die, but they also didn't know how to talk to her, and so they pretended nothing was wrong. During her treatment, their mom was often sick, and when she lost her hair the girls were more scared. It was just one more reminder that their mom was seriously ill. The girls weren't really looking forward to attending a support group for teens that their mom had asked them to check out, but when they went they were surprised to find out how great it was to talk to other kids their age dealing with the same issues.

If you know someone who has cancer, you may very well be faced with a dilemma. You may want to reach out to your friend, but on the other hand, what if you make things worse by doing or saying the wrong thing? That's why when someone is diagnosed with cancer, suddenly they find friends melt away. Soon nobody is calling or visiting, and the patient feels totally abandoned.

Try putting yourself in the cancer patient's position: Imagine how it might feel to have cancer. Most kids with cancer don't want to be treated as if they're "special." Being in the hospital or having to stay home a lot to rest can make you feel lonely and isolated.

Keep in touch. Most people with cancer like having their friends and family around, even if you don't stay long, or even if there doesn't seem to be much to say. If you're not sure whether to visit, ask.

If you don't live with the person, try to keep in touch—if you're like most kids, you're already on the Internet. E-mail the person or visit the person's personal Web page, MySpace or Facebook page, or blog—as often as you can. Sending cards or talking on the phone can help too. It may not take long, but it can cheer up a person with cancer to know friends and family haven't forgotten. People with cancer may need help with housework or everyday chores. Teens may find it helpful to talk to counselors or therapists or go to support groups and learn more about the emotional side of dealing with a health problem.

WHAT TO SAY TO SOMEONE WITH CANCER

One of the hardest things to deal with when someone you love has cancer is knowing what to say to that person. Sure, the person may be really sick with cancer, but that doesn't change who they are.

Be yourself. This may sound obvious or trite, but the most important thing you can do is to be yourself! Of course, it may be hard at first to "be yourself" when someone you care about has a serious disease. Just imagine to yourself what you *used* to talk about. You might try to "pretend" to yourself that the cancer never happened and just talk to the person as if that's the case. Soon you may be surprised at how easy it is to just be yourself around the other person.

Just remember that your friend is still the same person he or she always was. That person still wants to hear about the same things you two always talked about. Tell her what you're doing in school, what the cute guy said in chemistry class, or what the class clown did yesterday. Talk to him about soccer practice, who the coach yelled at, who's going out with the new girl. Recall old times and inside jokes. Bring along old pictures or yearbooks, or the latest school newspaper, so you can laugh together.

Many kids who have cancer say that the people they love suddenly treat them differently or stay away completely, and that upsets them. Can you imagine? You're dealing with a serious disease and all of a sudden your friends desert you!

One of the best things you can do is stay upbeat. Even with cancer, your friend wants to be able to laugh. Anything you can do to get the patient laughing will be a gift to that person.

Go ahead—talk about it. Afraid you'll say the wrong thing, so you don't say anything? It's *much* worse not to talk than to say the wrong thing, so go for it. If you're like most kids, the last thing you want to talk about with a friend who has cancer is their health situation. You may figure that your friend really doesn't want to talk about it. All too often, what happens is that the cancer becomes like an "elephant in the living room"—a huge topic that everybody pretends just isn't there, practically tripping over the elephant but never mentioning its presence.

In fact, most kids with cancer say that what really bothers them is that they *want* to talk about their cancer, but they think no one wants to hear. If you're a kid and you have cancer, it's really all you think about, all the time, but because other people worry that it would be too upsetting to discuss, nobody brings it up.

You'll be doing your friend a huge favor if you bring it up first. This takes the burden of introducing the subject off the patient and gives your friend a choice of either talking about the cancer or not. You can begin by gently asking your friend how he or she is feeling. Be honest—come right out and say: "Can we talk about your cancer, or would you rather not?"

If your friend really doesn't feel like it, he or she will probably tell you. If the friend says he'd like to chat, ask what the treatments are like. Ask if it hurts, and how he or she is coping. Go ahead and ask about your friend's feelings, and how she feels about being sick. Ask if she likes the doctors and nurses, if there's any special caregiver who really helps. If you're really brave, ask what the prognosis is. Ask about the daily schedule, or ask about losing her

---

Conversation Starters

It can be hard to know what to say to someone with cancer. Try some of these:

▶ "I'm sorry to hear that you're going through this."

▶ "Gosh, I can't believe it's cancer. How are you doing?"

▶ "I've been thinking about you."

hair—many types of cancer treatment cause this side effect, and nothing is more traumatic for a teenager (especially a girl) than being bald.

If you know a story about someone who survived the same type of cancer and is now living a long and healthy life, by all means, share. People with cancer need to know that there *are* people who survive this disease.

Your job is to be a good listener. Don't interrupt with your own stories or a tale about how your mom's aunt experienced something similar. Just listen to your friend. Don't worry if you break down and cry; tears mean you care, and don't be shocked or upset if your friend cries either. She's probably relieved to finally find someone who will actually allow her to discuss the "Big C." Odds are no one else has dared to ask anything about the illness.

If tears flow, just share a hug. There's nothing wrong with crying. It's an honest expression of emotion and entirely appropriate.

What not to say . . . Beware the fake optimism. If someone confesses to you that: "I'm afraid I'm going to die," don't immediately retort: "Oh, you're going to be just fine!" This discounts their true feelings with fake cheerfulness. If your friend is sharing a deep and frightening emotion, take a few breaths and listen before jumping in. It's much better to say something like: "It must be scary right now" instead of brushing aside their attempt to convey their fears.

Don't comment on your friend's appearance; odds are the person doesn't want to hear that he's looking really tired or awfully pale,

Don't Say . . .

> You should talk about it to everyone.

> I know just what you should do.

> You're such a hero!

> Why didn't you tell me sooner that you had cancer?

> You're so brave!

and while it may be tempting to say you know just how your friend feels, you probably don't unless you've also had cancer.

One of the worst things you can do is to trot out horror stories of other friends or family members who have had cancer and had horrible pain or died. It's amazing how common this is. Elizabeth's social worker gave her the name of another cancer survivor her own age to chat with on the phone, but when this girl called Elizabeth, she spent the first 10 minutes of the call telling a horrible story of how her own mother's cancer spread to the bones that required serial amputations—and the mom still died. This was so upsetting to Elizabeth that she felt worse than before the "support" call was made.

Make a concrete offer of help. Most people really want to be helpful, but they don't know what to do, so they end up saying something like: "Call me if you need anything!" or "Let me know if I can do something." This open-ended statement places the burden on the patient to try to figure out just exactly what you might be willing to do. A patient doesn't want to ask for favors so will likely never take you up on it.

Instead, make a specific offer: "Can I bring you your math assignments?" "Can I stay with your little sister for a few hours, so your mom can come visit you at the hospital?"

If it's your friend's mom or dad who has cancer, offer to babysit or bring over a pizza or a home-baked meal you know the family likes. Offer to mow the grass, run errands, or walk the dog. Ask your friend if he or she would like to go the movies or down to the mall for a couple of hours.

Don't be surprised if your offer of help is rejected. It's hard for most people to ask for, or accept, help from others. Just wait a couple of days and come up with another offer of help.

Make a plan for the future. It can help if you give your friend something to look forward to. Suggest a movie in a week or so, if the person is feeling up to it. Or offer to bring a CD and popcorn over for a "movie night" next weekend.

If you just can't face a friend . . . Sometimes kids find visiting a friend with cancer in the hospital to be just too traumatic. If you find yourself in this situation, try this: Make a gesture that doesn't require a face-to-face visit to break the ice. Send a great CD that you know your friend loves or a DVD of her favorite movie or TV series that was just released. Send flowers or a box of fruit. Lots of kids enjoy "care baskets" filled with little wrapped gifts—socks, CDs, books, funny

Lotsa Helping Hands

Lotsa Helping Hands (http://www.lotsahelpinghands.com) is a free, simple, immediate way for friends, family, colleagues, and neighbors to assist loved ones in need. It's an easy-to-use, private group calendar, specifically designed for organizing helpers, where everyone can pitch in with meal delivery, rides, and other tasks necessary for life to run smoothly during a crisis. Once a "coordinator" sets up the site, members are automatically notified by e-mail about needs that have been listed. You can see the group calendar and volunteer for whatever fits your own situation. Volunteers receive automatic confirmations and reminders of their commitments.

gifts, notes with a pen, lotions, lip gloss, books on tape, journals. If your friend is losing her hair, add a pretty scarf or a knitted cap. Even just a goofy card that you know will make him laugh is a good start. If you can't bring yourself to visit in person, keep sending similar items throughout your friend's illness.

COPING WITH YOUR FEELINGS

Of course, helping someone else cope with cancer doesn't mean you don't have some very serious issues of your own. It's natural to feel frightened, anxious, or even angry when someone you care about has cancer. You may feel sad, confused, uncomfortable, worried, unbelieving, guilty.

You'll need to cope with your own emotions about what it feels like having someone you love struggle with a disease that's very serious. It's not selfish to find you need help for yourself as well. Cancer never just affects one person in a family or community—it affects everyone that person loves.

Having so many fears and uncomfortable feelings can make it hard to talk to even the most supportive family members and friends. This is why support groups for teens are so important—they can help you feel less alone and help you deal better with the uncertainties and challenges that cancer brings. Support groups can give you a chance to meet and discuss ways to cope with the illness. You'll find that some support groups are designed just for family members and friends of patients.

They may be led by a mental health professional such as a psychiatrist, psychologist, or social worker, or by cancer patients or survivors themselves. Many groups are free, but some charge a fee. (Some health insurance policies will cover the cost.) At a support group, you can expect to find other kids your age whose family members or friends are coping with cancer, and everyone gets to talk about how this makes them feel. Because everyone at the meeting is in the same situation, they all share pretty much of the same fears and worries. Participants may be able to share what helped them cope or offer tips on how to handle various situations.

Where to find them. Many hospitals and organizations offer support groups for family members or friends of people with cancer. The National Cancer Institute offers a fact sheet listing many cancer-concerned organizations that can provide information about support groups. This fact sheet is available on the Internet at http://www. cancer.gov/cancertopics/factsheet/support/organizations, or you can order one from the Cancer Information Service ([800] 422-6237). Some of these organizations provide information on their Web sites about contacting support groups.

Anyone who works with cancer patients—doctors, nurses, or social workers—may also have information about local support groups. Most hospitals have social services departments that can give you information about these programs. You can also find notices about support groups in your local newspaper or Yellow Pages. Appendix 1 also lists organizations that offer support groups.

HANDLING YOUR FRIENDS' CONCERN

If a family member has cancer, your good friends will probably want to talk to you about it because they care, but kids this age may not always know exactly what to say, and they may feel awkward. The more open you can be, the more at ease they'll probably feel.

Of course, sometimes you just may not want to talk about the whole thing. Just dealing with it at home is probably pretty tough—you may feel that you just want to forget the fact that a family member has cancer when you're with your friends or away from the house. It's perfectly normal to want to escape the stress of serious disease.

Whether or not you want to talk about it is also up to you. If you really don't want to talk, it's okay to tell your friends: "I appreciate your concern but I'd rather not talk about it right now." Teens often feel as if they're inundated with "cancer talk" at home, and many teens just want to be treated like all the other kids.

SHOWING YOUR SUPPORT

If you feel as if you'd like to do *more* for your friend or family member with cancer, there is a whole host of ways that you can donate your time or money to help in the fight against cancer.

Volunteer. You might consider volunteering at a hospital or clinic that treats people with cancer. Volunteering is an excellent way to show your support (although there may be age limits—check with the hospital).

The Colleges Against Cancer program allows college students, faculty, and staff to work together to bring American Cancer Society programs and services to college communities nationwide. You can work with CAC through grassroots advocacy, prevention and early detection education, Relay For Life, and activities honoring cancer survivors. For more information about how CAC chapters make a difference, visit http://www.cancer.org/docroot/VOL/Content/VOL_2_Colleges_vs_Cancer.asp.

If you're interested in volunteering in other American Cancer Society programs in your community, visit the ACS Web site to learn more at: http://www.cancer.org/docroot/vol/content/VOL_1_1_How_To_Get_Involved_Locally.asp.

Donate blood. If you're at least age 17 (or 16 in some states), you may donate blood in a patient's name (if the person needs blood).

Advertise your support. You also can show your support for a variety of cancers by wearing a Lance Armstrong LiveStrong bracelet or the pink ribbon of breast cancer supporters.

Donate. You may not have a lot of money—hey, you're just a kid!—but you can still give something to help in the fight against cancer. You may want to make a one-time donation or pledge to make regular, repeated donations throughout the year. You can specify that your gift honor a special occasion in your loved one's life—a holiday, anniversary, graduation, or birthday—or to celebrate the memory of someone who died from cancer. You can donate to the American Cancer Society or to an organization dedicated to a specific type of cancer.

Build a memorial site. The American Cancer Society offers a "Mosaic of Memories" in which friends or family members of someone who has died from cancer can create a Web page as a tribute to the person. To learn more, visit http://www.acsevents. org/site/pp.asp?c = feIOLOOnGlF&b = 871941.

Participate in activities. You can get involved in the fight against cancer by participating in fund-raising efforts and helping with activities in your area for the ACS or another cancer organization. The American Cancer Society alone has a host of activities in which you may want to participate, including Daffodil Days, Relay for Life, Making Strides Against Breast Cancer, Team ACS, and Coaches vs. Cancer. Visit the ACS Web site at: http://www.cancer.org/docroot/PAR/PAR_ 0.asp to learn more about these programs.

Many cancer-related organizations offer tournaments, galas, runs, and other activities to help raise money to fight cancer.

WHAT YOU NEED TO KNOW

- ▶ When dealing with someone who has cancer, the most important thing you can do is to be yourself.
- ▶ Many kids who have cancer say that one of the worst things about the disease is that the people they love suddenly treat them differently or stay away completely.
- ▶ Don't say you know what they're feeling or offer false "just be positive" comments. Don't tell scary stories about other people you knew who had cancer.
- ▶ Don't treat a person with cancer as if he or she is "special" or breakable.
- ▶ Don't ignore a friend's cancer.
- ▶ It's natural to feel frightened, anxious, sad, confused, uncomfortable, worried, unbelieving, guilty, or even angry when someone you care about has cancer.
- ▶ Teen support groups for friends and families of patients are important because they can help you feel less alone and help you deal better with the uncertainties and challenges that cancer brings.
- ▶ Whether or not you want to talk to friends about the fact that a family member has cancer is up to you.

10 ▎▎▎

Paying for Care

If you or someone in your family has cancer, the last thing you want to have to worry about is how you're going to pay for care. Yet in the United States today, some families don't have health insurance. Others have problems meeting expenses that aren't covered by insurance (such as wigs, which most health insurers don't cover). Financial problems can be scary, but luckily there are lots of groups and organizations that can help. There's no need to go without treatment, medication, or necessary services because of an inability to pay.

BASIC HEALTH-CARE COVERAGE

If your family has a good health insurance policy, that's terrific, but some families can't afford coverage, and their jobs don't offer it. Many families make too much to qualify for state-subsidized health insurance (Medicaid) but not enough to pay for private insurance. Others just have high deductibles or lots of things that may be needed that aren't covered by health-care policies.

Fortunately, every state has a special program called "Insure Kids Now" for infants, children, and teens, available to children in working families, even families that include individuals with a variety of immigration status. For little or no cost, this insurance pays for doctor visits, prescription medicines, hospitalizations, and much more. Kids who don't currently have health insurance are likely to be eligible, even if their parents are working. Each state has different eligibility rules, but in most states, uninsured children 18 years old and younger, whose families earn up to $34,100 a year (for a family of four), are eligible. To find out more about your individual state's rules, you or your parents can call (877) KIDS-NOW or go online to http://www. insurekidsnow.gov/states.htm. For more information (in Spanish and English) about immigration status and insurance, visit http://www. ask.hrsa.gov/detail.cfm?id = HRS00291.

MEDICAID

Eligible families who are below income limits (which vary depending on how many people are in the family) may already know all about Medicaid, the state-run public health program that covers payment for a variety of health-care services.

Medicaid does not pay money to your parents but sends payments directly to your health-care providers. Depending on your state's rules, you may also be asked to pay a small part of the cost (it's called a co-payment) for some services. Each state sets its own guidelines regarding eligibility and services, but all states must cover some benefits, including hospital and outpatient care, doctor services, and home health services.

Your parents can get more information about their eligibility at your local welfare and medical assistance offices, to see exactly what's covered where you live and what the income limits are. Or you can check out the Medicaid Web site at: http://www.CMS.gov.

Medicaid for Breast and Cervical Cancer Patients

The Breast and Cervical Cancer Treatment Act of 2000 extends Medicaid coverage for treatment to women who have been screened and diagnosed through the National Breast and Cervical Cancer Early Detection Program in states that have agreed to provide this service. For more information, call **(888) 842-6355** or visit their Web site: http://www.cdc.gov/cancer/nbccedp/index.htm.

EMERGENCY ROOM COVERAGE

If you or a member of your family has cancer, there may be times that an emergency room visit is necessary. If you need help with hospital expenses, ask to speak to a financial counselor in the business office of the hospital. They can help you develop a monthly payment plan. If your parents don't have any health insurance coverage or Medicaid, you should know that anyone who comes to the emergency department asking for examination or treatment for a medical condition must be examined to determine if it's an emergency. It's guaranteed by federal law. If the person is having a true emergency, the hospital must either provide free treatment until the person is better or transfer the person to another hospital. Almost every hospital in the country must abide by this law.

If you or a family member is having a reaction to chemotherapy or another treatment, or seems to be developing an infection (especially while undergoing chemo), you should never think twice about going to the ER. They will not turn you away.

OTHER CANCER-RELATED FINANCIAL HELP

The following organizations offer a range of financial services to patients with cancer in the United States.

American Cancer Society
1599 Clifton Road NE
Atlanta, GA 30329-4251
(800) ACS-2345
http://www.cancer.org/docroot/home/index.asp
Local American Cancer Society offices offer reimbursement for expenses related to cancer treatment. The exact type of assistance that is available varies by office. For more information, call your local ACS office. You can find the number in the phone book, online, or by visiting the national ACS Web site and typing in your zip code.

CancerCare Assist
275 Seventh Avenue
New York, NY 10001
(212) 712-8080
(800) 813-4673
http://www.cancercare.org/get_help
CancerCare administers many different support programs for patients with cancer. For more than 60 years, CancerCare has provided

*financial assistance to help with some types of costs. Their social
workers and case managers are well trained in financial issues
and will work closely with patients to get them the help they
need. Patients who need financial assistance should call the above
number to find out if there is an appropriate program.*

National Cancer Institute Cancer Information Service
(800) 4CANCER
http://www.cancer.gov
*The National Cancer Institute's Cancer Information Service can
direct you to local programs designed to help cancer patients with
financial problems as well.*

MEDICATION

Chemotherapy drugs are extremely expensive, and almost all patients
with cancer must take several different types. The exact cost of chemotherapy varies depending on what kinds and how much of the
medicine is used and how long treatment will be. Treatment costs
also depend on whether the drugs are given at home, in a clinic or a
doctor's office, or as an inpatient.

Most health insurance policies cover at least part of the cost of
many kinds of chemotherapy, but if your family doesn't have insurance, there are organizations that can help with the cost of chemotherapy and transportation. Have your mom or dad ask a nurse or
social worker about these organizations.

If the patient is considering participating in a new treatment study,
these medicines are often given free of charge. If the treatment isn't
free, however, some insurers won't cover certain medicine costs if the
drug is considered "experimental." Your doctor can work with you to
try to help you. Many insurance companies handle new treatments on
a case-by-case basis rather than having a general policy.

For other medications, your doctor may be able to offer you free
samples on a limited basis.

PATIENT ASSISTANCE PROGRAMS

Many people don't realize that most drug companies have special
patient assistance programs that provide free medications to patients
who can't afford them. Patient assistance programs also may be called
indigent drug programs, charitable drug programs, or medication assistance programs. Most of the best-known and most prescribed drugs
can be found in these programs, and all of the major drug companies

If You're Turned Down for Free Medication . . .

It's up to each drug company to decide if someone can have free medication, and sometimes people are turned down. In that case, the best thing to do is to have your parents ask your doctor, social worker, or health-care advocate to appeal directly to the manager of the patient assistance program. A letter followed by a phone call may help.

have patient assistance programs. However, every company has different eligibility and application requirements. Generally, individuals must have incomes under 200 percent of the Federal Poverty Level (that's an income below $25,660 for a family of two), can't have prescription coverage from any public or private source, and must be a U.S. resident or citizen. Some companies require that the patient has no health insurance. Typically, a doctor's note is needed to apply, along with proof of financial need or a letter outlining the lack of health insurance or prescription drug benefits.

Individual drug companies usually list their patient assistance programs online, so if you know the medication you need and you know the company that produces it, you can simply do an Internet search for the company's name and check out their Web site. Or, you can check out one of the many Web sites that provide information about patient assistance programs:

Free Medicine Foundation
P.O. Box 125
Doniphan, MO 63935
(573) 996-3333
http://www.freemedicinefoundation.com
*This foundation helped more than 7.6 million patients obtain more
    than 11 million free prescriptions in 2005. Qualifications range
    from a family income below the national poverty level up to
    $38,000, although in some cases families with annual incomes as*

high as $60,000 can receive free drugs. Each sponsored drug has its own eligibility criteria.

The Medicine Program
http://www.themedicineprogram.com
This program offers a unique discounted prescription drug program that is free and available to anyone interested in lowering the cost of their medications with no minimum eligibility requirements. To obtain a free prescription card, you simply print out a copy at the Web site listed above, present it at one of more than 35,000 participating pharmacies, and save up to 60 percent on medication.

NeedyMeds
120 Western Avenue
Gloucester, MA 01930
(215) 625-9609
http://www.needymeds.com
NeedyMeds is a source of information about patient assistance programs and other programs that help low-income people obtain health supplies and equipment. Free information is available at this site, but a printed version of the data (called the NeedyMeds Manual) is available for a fee, which contains the information on the Web site for those who find it easier to use a printed version.

Partnership for Prescription Assistance
(888) 4PPA-NOW [477-2669]
http://www.pparx.org/Intro.php
The Partnership for Prescription Assistance is a joint venture of the American Academy of Family Physicians, the American Autoimmune Related Diseases Association, the Lupus Foundation of America, the NAACP, the National Alliance for Hispanic Health, the National Medical Association, and a number of drug companies, health-care providers, and community groups. The partnership is dedicated to helping qualified patients without prescription coverage get the medicines they need, at either a reduced price or no cost at all.

Patient Advocate Foundation
Co-Pay Relief Program
(866) 512-3861
http://www.copays.org
This program provides limited payment assistance for medicines to insured patients who financially and medically qualify.

RxAssist

http://www.rxassist.org

RxAssist is a Web site that offers a comprehensive database of patient assistance programs run by pharmaceutical companies, to provide free medications to people who cannot afford to buy their medicines. The site also offers practical tools, news, and articles so that health-care professionals and patients can find the information they need. RxAssist was created by Volunteers in Health Care, a national, nonprofit resource center for health-care programs working with the uninsured.

CANADIAN MEDICATIONS

It's also possible to save money on prescription medications by buying them online from Canada. Although the U.S. government frowns on the practice because of safety concerns, consumer advocates say it's a sensible choice for people on tight budgets. Several reputable Web sites have been established that are linked with U.S. state governments.

ILLINOIS, KANSAS, MISSOURI, VERMONT, WISCONSIN:

I-SaveRx

http://www.i-saverx.net

People in Illinois, Kansas, Missouri, Vermont, or Wisconsin can participate in I-SaveRx, a mail-order pharmacy program developed by the governors of the above five states to provide mail-order access to cheaper prescription drugs from Canada, the United Kingdom, and Ireland. Any resident of these five states can participate.

MINNESOTA:

Minnesota RXConnect

http://www.state.mn.us/portal/mn/jsp/home.do?agency = Rx

The Minnesota governor established a Web site to help residents buy medications from Canada and the United Kingdom at a more affordable price.

NEW HAMPSHIRE:

http://www.egov.nh.gov/medicine%2Dcabinet

Listing a number of helpful sites on their official Web site, the state of New Hampshire also offers a link for residents to visit: CanadaDrugs.com.

NORTH DAKOTA:

http://www.governor.state.nd.us/prescription-drug.html
North Dakota's state Web page on Canadian drugs offers detailed explanations and links to Web sites to help residents import medications.

WHAT YOU NEED TO KNOW

▶ Every state has a special program offering health insurance to kids and teens.
▶ Medicaid is a state program that offers health-care coverage to people under certain income limits.
▶ You must be examined and treated at an emergency room if you're sick, even if you can't pay or don't have insurance.
▶ A number of companies offer free or reduced-priced medications if you don't have health insurance and you meet income limits.
▶ Certain states offer Web sites explaining how to obtain medications at lower prices from Canada.

APPENDIX 1

National Organizations

This appendix includes some of the national organizations that provide support for cancer patients.

AIR TRANSPORTATION (See FINANCIAL HELP)

AMPUTATION
American Amputee Foundation, Inc.
P.O. Box 250218
Hillcrest Station
Little Rock, AR 72225
(501) 666-2523
info@americanamputee.org
http://www.americanamputee.org/
Organization that provides information and referrals to amputees and their families and prints a National Resource Directory every two years as a source for amputees and professionals in the amputee-related field. People without financial means are given prosthesis devices. The agency makes referrals to different support groups and publishes a biannual newsletter. If you have been denied SSI, if your rehabilitation isn't working, or if you're not old enough, this organization will help you.

APPEARANCE
Let's Face It
P.O. Box 29972
Bellingham, WA 98228
(360) 676-7325
http://www.faceit.org
A nonprofit support network that links people with facial disfigurement and all who care for them to resources that can

94

enrich their lives. Services include an annual resource directory, self-help network book, and phone consultations.

Look Good . . . Feel Better
CTFA Foundation
1101 17th Street NW
Washington, DC 20036
(800) 395-5665
(202) 331-1770
http://www.lookgoodfeelbetter.org
This program helps cancer patients improve their appearance during treatment. LGFB offers workshops across the country, often in conjunction with the local American Cancer Society chapters. Services include makeup kits; free program materials; patient education; counseling; hair care, skin care, and makeup tips; voluntary services.

Look Good . . . Feel Better for Teens
CTFA Foundation
1101 17th Street NW
Washington, DC 20036
(800) 395-5665
(202) 331-1770
http://www.lookgoodfeelbetter.org/audience/teens/program.htm
Look Good . . . Feel Better for Teens is a hospital-based public service program created by the Cosmetic, Toiletry, and Fragrance Association (CTFA) and its partners to help girls and guys ages 13–17 deal with the appearance, health, and social side effects of cancer treatment. Launched in 1996, the program now offers on-site sessions in 16 cities, as well as the 2bMe Web site at http://www.2bme.org/2bMe.html. 2bMe is the online component of Look Good . . . Feel Better for Teens. The information-packed Web site covers all the nonmedical stuff teens with cancer wonder about— from skin and hair to fitness and friends—and there are interactive style finder quizzes, how-to demos, and fashion slide shows. 2bMe is also recommended by Starbright World, the powerful hospital-to-hospital intranet for children with serious illnesses.

National Foundation for Facial Reconstruction
317 East 34th Street, Suite 901
New York, NY 10016
(212) 263-6656
http://www.nffr.org

NFFR is a voluntary organization aiding the rehabilitation of people suffering from facial disfigurement. Services include physician, hospital, or clinic referrals for those unable to afford private reconstructive surgical care.

BLADDER CANCER

American Urological Association (AUA)
1000 Corporate Boulevard
Linthicum, MD 21090
(866) 746-4282
(410) 689-3700
http://www.auanet.org
The American Urological Association Foundation was established to support and promote research, patient/public education, and advocacy to improve the prevention, detection, treatment, and cure of urologic disease.

BONE MARROW TRANSPLANTS

Blood & Marrow Transplant Information Network
2900 Skokie Valley Road, Suite B
Highland Park, IL 60035
(847) 433-3313
(888) 597-7674
http://www.marrow.org
A nonprofit organization that provides publications and support services to bone marrow, peripheral blood stem cell, and cord blood transplant patients and survivors. It publishes a quarterly newsletter (Blood & Marrow Transplant Newsletter) *for bone marrow, peripheral stem cell, and cord blood transplant patients; a resource directory; a "patient-to-survivor" telephone link; and a 157-page book describing physical and emotional aspects of marrow and stem cell transplantation. A second book,* Mira's Month *($5), helps prepare young children for a parent's transplant. Additional resources for the public include a directory of transplant centers, with information on types and number of transplants performed and diseases treated, and an attorney list, to help resolve insurance problems.*

The Bone Marrow Foundation
70 East 55th Street, 20th Floor
New York, NY 10022

(212) 838-3029
(800) 365-1336
http://www.bonemarrow.org
*Provides eligible transplant candidates with financial assistance
limited to helping defray the cost of ancillary services needed to
ensure proper care during the transplant procedure, as well as in
pre- and post-transplant treatment phases.*

Bone Marrow Transplant Family Support Network
P.O. Box 845
Avon, CT 06001
(800) 826-9376
*A national telephone support network for patients and their families.
Services: Referrals; BMT information; counseling; children's
services; health insurance information. The network answers
questions raised by the person calling and will connect newly
diagnosed patients with a recovered BMT patient who is the same
age, has the same diagnosis, stage of disease, etc.*

National Bone Marrow Transplant Link
20411 West 12 Mile Road, Suite 108
Southfield, MI 48076
(800) 546-5268
nbmtlink@aol.com
http://www.nbmtlink.org
*This group operates a 24-hour toll-free number and provides peer
support to bone marrow transplant (BMT) patients and their
families. It also serves as an information center for prospective
BMT patients as well as a resource for health professionals.
Educational publications, brochures, and videos are available.
Staff can respond to calls in Spanish.*

National Marrow Donor Program (NMDP)
3001 Broadway Street NE, Suite 500
Minneapolis, MN 55413-1753
(612) 627-5800
(800) 627-7692
http://www.marrow.org
*The National Marrow Donor Program, funded by the federal
government, was created to improve the effectiveness of the
search for bone marrow donors. It keeps a registry of potential
bone marrow donors and provides free information on bone
marrow transplantation, peripheral blood stem cell transplant,*

*and unrelated donor stem cell transplant, including the use of
umbilical cord blood. The NMDP's Office of Patient Advocacy
assists transplant patients and their physicians through the donor
search and transplant process by providing information, referrals,
support, and advocacy.*

BRAIN TUMOR
American Brain Tumor Association (ABTA)
2720 River Road
Des Plaines, IL 60018
(847) 827-9910
(800) 886-2282
info@abta.org
http://www.abta.org
*The ABTA funds brain tumor research and provides information to
help patients make educated decisions about their health care. The
ABTA offers printed materials about the research and treatment
of brain tumors and provides listings of physicians, treatment
facilities, and support groups throughout the country. A limited
selection of Spanish-language publications is available.*

Brain Tumor Foundation for Children, Inc. (BTFC)
1835 Savoy Drive, Suite 316
Atlanta, GA 30341
(770) 458-5554
http://www.btfcgainc.org
*This nonprofit organization provides information and patient services
for children with brain tumors. Services include family support
and education programs, public awareness and information
activities, a telephone support network, and regular meetings and
recreational events for children and their families. BTFC also funds
research.*

The Brain Tumor Society
124 Watertown Street, Suite 3-H
Watertown, MA 02472
(617) 924-9997
(800) 770-8287
info@tbts.org
http://www.tbts.org
*The Brain Tumor Society provides information about brain tumors
and related conditions for patients and their families. They offer*

a patient/family network, educational publications, funding for research projects, and access to support groups for patients.

Children's Brain Tumor Foundation (CBTF)
274 Madison Avenue, Suite 1301
New York, NY 10016
(212) 448-9494
(866) 228-4673
info@cbtf.org
http://www.cbtf.org
The CBTF is a nonprofit organization that funds research and provides support, education, and advocacy for children with brain and spinal cord tumors and their families. It also provides educational materials (including a Spanish-language publication) and cosponsors conferences and seminars for families, survivors, and health-care professionals that offer the latest information about research, treatments, and strategies for living. Through CBTF's Parent-to-Parent Network, families share their experiences with others in similar situations.

The Dana Alliance for Brain Initiatives
745 Fifth Avenue, Suite 700
New York, NY 10151
The Dana Alliance, a nonprofit organization of 150 neuroscientists, was formed to help provide information about the personal and public benefits of brain research.

The Guardian Brain Foundation
P.O. Box 1216
Bellmore, NY 11710
(516) 679-5075
info@guardianbrain.com
http://www.guardianbrain.com
The mission of the Guardian Brain Foundation is to help advance neuroscience research, provide support services, and to improve quality of life for adults and children diagnosed with injuries and tumors of the brain.

National Brain Tumor Foundation (NBTF)
22 Battery Street, Suite 612
San Francisco, CA 94111–5520
(415) 834-9970
(800) 934-2873

nbtf@braintumor.org

http://www.braintumor.org

The NBTF provides patients and their families with information on how to cope with their brain tumors. This organization conducts national and regional conferences, publishes printed materials for patients and family members, provides access to a national network of patient support groups, and assists in answering patient inquiries. The NBTF also awards grants to fund research. Staffers are available to answer calls in Spanish, and some Spanish-language publications are available.

National Institute of Neurological Disorders and Stroke
NIH Neurological Institute
P.O. Box 5801
Bethesda, MD 20824
(800) 352-9424
This federal institute conducts and supports research on many serious diseases affecting the brain.

BREAST CANCER
About Breast Health
315 East Broadway, Suite 305
Louisville, KY 40202
(502) 629-6950
info@AboutBreastHealth.com
http://www.aboutbreasthealth.com
A resource for breast cancer patients or other concerned persons, this site provides general information, an informative Frequently Asked Question list (FAQ), and a portal for people to contact physicians and support groups.

ENCOREPlus
YWCA of the USA
Office of Women's Health Advocacy
1015 18th Street NW, Suite 700
Washington, DC 20036
(202) 467-0801
(800) 953-7587
cgould@ywca.org
http://www.ywca.org
ENCOREPlus is the YWCA's discussion and exercise program for women who have had breast cancer surgery. It is designed to help

*restore physical strength and emotional well-being. Any local
branch of the YWCA, listed in the phone directory, can provide
more information about ENCOREPlus.*

Judges and Lawyers Breast Cancer Alert (JALBCA)
369 Madison Avenue, PMB 424
New York, NY 10128
(212) 683-6630
http://www.jalbca.org
*JALBCA is a confidential hotline for judges, lawyers, and law
students who have been diagnosed with breast cancer.*

Living Beyond Breast Cancer (LBBC)
10 East Athens Avenue, Suite 204
Ardmore, PA 19003
(610) 645-4567
(888) 753-5222 (Survivors' Helpline)
mail@lbbc.org
http://www.lbbc.org
*The LBBC is an educational organization that aims to empower
women with breast cancer to live as long as possible with the best
quality of life. The LBBC offers an interactive message board and
information about upcoming conferences and teleconferences on
its Web site. In addition, the organization has a toll-free Survivors'
Helpline, a Young Survivors Network for women diagnosed with
breast cancer who are age 45 or younger, and outreach programs
for medically underserved communities. The LBBC also offers a
quarterly educational newsletter and a book for African-American
women living with breast cancer.*

National Alliance of Breast Cancer Organizations (NABCO)
9 East 37th Street, 10th Floor
New York, NY 10016
(888) 80-NABCO
(212) 719-0154
http://www.nabco.org
*NABCO provides information about breast cancer and acts as an
advocate for the legislative concerns of breast cancer patients and
survivors.*

National Breast and Cervical Cancer Early Detection Program
Centers for Disease Control and Prevention (CDC)
4770 Buford Highway NE, MS K64

Atlanta, GA 30341
(888) 842-6355
http://www.cdc.gov/cancer/nbccedp
This program of the CDC provides screening services, including
clinical breast examinations, mammograms, pelvic examinations,
and Pap tests, to underserved women. The program also funds
post-screening diagnostic services, such as surgical consultation
and biopsy, to ensure that all women with abnormal results
receive timely and adequate referrals. Services include referrals,
public information and education programs, and appropriate
surveillance and epidemiological systems.

National Breast Cancer Coalition (NBCC)
1101 17th Street NW, Suite 1300
Washington, DC 20036
(202) 296-7477
(800) 622-2838
info@stopbreastcancer.org
http://www.natlbcc.org
The NBCC is a breast cancer advocacy group that educates and trains
individuals to become advocates who effectively influence public
policies that affect breast cancer research and treatment. It also
promotes breast cancer research and works to improve access to
high-quality breast cancer screening, diagnosis, and treatment for
all women.

Reach to Recovery
American Cancer Society (ACS)
1599 Clifton Road NE
Atlanta, GA 30329-4251
(404) 320-3333
(800) 227-2345
http://www.cancer.org
The Reach to Recovery Program is a rehabilitation program for men
and women who have or have had breast cancer. The program
helps breast cancer patients meet the physical, emotional, and
cosmetic needs related to their disease and its treatment.

Sisters Network, Inc.
8787 Woodway Drive, Suite 4206
Houston, TX 77063
(866) 781-1808
sisnet4@aol.com

http://www.sistersnetworkinc.org
*Sisters Network seeks to increase local and national attention
to the impact that breast cancer has in the African-American
community. All chapters are run by breast cancer survivors and
receive volunteer assistance from community leaders and associate
members. The services provided by Sisters Network include
individual/group support, community education, advocacy, and
research. The national headquarters serves as a resource and
referral base for survivors, clinical trials, and private/government
agencies. Teleconferences are held to update chapters with the
latest information and share new ideas. An educational brochure
designed for underserved women is available. In addition, a
national African-American breast cancer survivors newsletter is
distributed to survivors, medical facilities, government agencies,
organizations, and churches nationwide.*

The Susan G. Komen Breast Cancer Foundation
5005 LBJ Freeway, Suite 250
P.O. Box 650309
Dallas, TX 75244
(972) 855-1600
(800) 462-9273
http://www.komen.org
*A toll-free breast cancer helpline ([800] I'M AWARE) is answered
by trained volunteers whose lives have been personally touched
by breast cancer. Breast health and breast cancer materials are
available. Also includes information on Komen Race for the Cure.*

Women's Healthcare Educational Network, Inc. (WHEN)
P.O. Box 5061
Tiffin, OH 44883
(800) 991-8877
http://www.whenusa.org
*An organization of independent businesses that specializes in
serving women who have had breast surgery. The network offers
information and referrals to physicians, nurses, and managed care
providers and provides specialty items like wigs, maternity and
nursing products, compression therapy products (for pain relief),
and prostheses.*

Women's Information Network Against Breast Cancer
536 South Second Avenue, Suite K
Covina, CA 91723-3043

(866) 294-6222
(626) 332-2255
http://www.winabc.org
This national nonprofit organization offers information, resources,
  peer support, and referral sources for breast cancer patients and
  their families through telephone counseling, mail support, and
  community outreach.

Y-ME National Breast Cancer Organization, Inc.
212 West Van Buren, Suite 500
Chicago, IL 60607
(800) 221-2141 (English)
(800) 986-9505 (Spanish)
http://www.y-me.org
A nonprofit consumer-oriented organization that provides
  information, referral, and emotional support to individuals
  concerned about or diagnosed with breast cancer. Hotline is
  staffed by trained counselors and volunteers who have experienced
  breast cancer and offer peer support. Services include referrals,
  educational programs, counseling, rehabilitation, advocacy, and
  health insurance information. Y-ME also offers a Men's Support
  Line Monday through Friday 9 A.M. to 5 P.M. CST. Men can call
  the Y-ME 800 number and request to speak to a male counselor.
  The counselor most closely matched in experience to the caller will
  return the call within 24 hours.

The Young Survival Coalition
Box 528, 52A Carmine Street
New York, NY 10014
(212) 916-7667
http://www.youngsurvival.org
This organization focuses on the issues and challenges faced by
  women aged 40 and under who are diagnosed with breast cancer.

CAMPS
Camp Adventure American Cancer Society
75 Davids Drive
Hauppauge, NY 11788
(631) 436-7070
Camp Adventure is a one-week sleepaway camp program for children
  with cancer and their brothers and sisters, ages six to 18. It offers the
  fun-filled camp each August on the shores of eastern Long Island.

Children's Oncology Camping Association (C.O.C.A.) International
1221 Center Street, Suite 12
Des Moines, IA 50309
(515) 243-6239
mark@childrenscancerprograms.com
http://www.coca-intl.org
C.O.C.A. is an international assembly of people providing camping programs for children with cancer. In 1982, C.O.C.A., Children's Oncology Camps of America, was founded by a dozen pioneer oncology camps; today, C.O.C.A. consists of more than 65 member camps from within the United States. There are also several member camps from the Canadian provinces and several camps located on faraway continents such as Australia, New Zealand, and Europe. C.O.C.A. International meets annually at a conference that is hosted by a member camp. Their Web site offers links, resources, and a listing of member camps.

Hole in the Wall Gang Camp
565 Ashford Center Road
Ashford, CT 06278
(860) 429-3444
http://www.holeinthewallgang.org
Started and funded by actor Paul Newman, this summer camp is designed for children with cancer and/or serious blood diseases. The camp provides year-round activities for campers and other seriously ill children and their siblings at camp and in their own communities.

CANADIAN GROUPS
CanSurmount
(888) 939-3333 (Canada)
(800) ACS-2345 (U.S.A.)
This Canadian organization affiliated with the Canadian Cancer Society offers education and support for patients and family members. The group tries to match volunteers who have survived cancer with patients who are in the hospital. Services provided in English and French.

CANCER
AMC Cancer Research Center
1600 Pierce Street
Denver, CO 80214

(303) 233-6501
(800) 525-3777
http://www.amc.org

A nonprofit research institute dedicated to the prevention of cancer. Provides up-to-date facts about all aspects of cancer as well as personal assistance from counselors trained and experienced in dealing with the fear, confusion, conflicts, and other problems often associated with the disease. All staff are paid professionals with degrees in counseling or related health areas. Through its Cancer Information and Counseling Line (CICL), a toll-free phone service, members of the general public have access to the latest information on cancer prevention, detection, diagnosis, treatment, and rehabilitation, including the Physicians' Data Query (PDQ), a database of research studies and treatment protocols from the nation's cancer centers. The service mails out thousands of free brochures and other literature every year and helps put callers in touch with cancer-related resources in their communities. In addition, AMC-CRC funds research.

American Cancer Society (ACS)

1599 Clifton Road NE
Atlanta, GA 30329-4251
(404) 320-3333
(800) 227-2345
http://www.cancer.org

The ACS is a voluntary organization that offers a variety of services to patients and their families. The ACS also supports research, provides printed materials, and conducts educational programs. Staff can accept calls and distribute publications in Spanish. A local ACS unit may be listed in the white pages of the phone book under "American Cancer Society."

American Institute for Cancer Research (AICR)

1759 R Street NW
Washington, DC 20009
(800) 843-8114
(202) 328-7744
aicrweb@aicr.org
http://www.aicr.org

The institute provides information about cancer prevention, particularly through diet and nutrition, and offers a toll-free nutrition hotline, pen pal support network, and funding of research grants. Spanish language publications are available.

American Society of Clinical Oncology (ASCO)
1900 Duke Street, Suite 200
Alexandria, VA 22314
(703) 299-0150
asco@asco.org
http://www.asco.org
*ASCO is a nonprofit organization founded in 1964 as a way to
improve cancer care and prevention and ensure that all patients
with cancer receive care of the highest quality. More than 23,000
oncology health-care practitioners belong to ASCO, representing
all oncology disciplines (medical, radiologic, and surgical
oncology) and subspecialties. As the world's leading professional
organization representing physicians who treat people with cancer,
ASCO is committed to advancing the education of oncologists
and other oncology professionals, to advocating for policies that
provide access to high-quality cancer care, and to supporting both
the clinical trials system and the need for increased clinical and
translational research.*

Cancer.com
http://www.cancer.com
*Developed by Ortho Biotech Products, Cancer.com is a portal
aggregating links to cancer-related Web sites and online tools. The
information is organized by topic, and there are special sections
for caregivers and health-care professionals.*

CancerCare, Inc.
275 Seventh Avenue
New York, NY 10001
(212) 712-8080
(800) 813-4673
info@cancercare.org
http://www.cancercare.org
*CancerCare is a national nonprofit agency that offers free support,
information, financial assistance, and practical help to people with
cancer and their loved ones. Services are provided by oncology
social workers and are available in person, over the phone, and
through the agency's Web site. A section of the CancerCare Web
site and some publications are available in Spanish, and staff can
respond to calls and e-mails in Spanish. CancerCare also operates
the AVONCares Program for Medically Underserved Women,
which provides financial assistance to low-income, under- and
uninsured, underserved women throughout the country who need*

*supportive services (transportation, child care, and home care)
related to the treatment of breast and cervical cancers.*

Cancer Consultants
(208) 727-6880
ldubose@cancerconsultants.com
http://www.cancerconsultants.com
*Cancer Consultants is dedicated to providing comprehensive
prevention and treatment information, up-to-date news, and
clinical trials listings for cancer patients and their families. The
service is part of the Cancer Information Network.*

Cancer Information and Counseling Line (CICL)
AMC Cancer Research Center
1600 Pierce Street
Denver, CO 80214
(800) 525-3777
ciclhelp@amc.org
http://www.amc.org/html/info/h_info_cicl.html
*The CICL, part of the Psychosocial Program of the AMC Cancer
Research Center, is a toll-free service for cancer patients, their family
members and friends, cancer survivors, and the general public.
Professional counselors provide up-to-date medical information,
emotional support through short-term counseling, and resource
referrals to callers nationwide between the hours of 8:30 A.M. and
5:00 P.M. MST, Monday through Friday. Individuals may also submit
questions about cancer and request resources via e-mail.*

Cancer Information Service
Building 31, Room 10A16
9000 Rockville Pike
Bethesda, MD 20892
(800) 4 CANCER
(301) 402-5874
http://www.icic.nci.nih.gov
*This nationwide network was founded by the National Cancer
Institute (NCI). Calls are routed to local CIS offices, where trained
cancer information specialists answer virtually any question on
cancer. More than 100 free pamphlets are available; the CIS is
committed to increasing the public's awareness through outreach.
The CIS outreach coordinator is available to groups to help you set
up your own education programs.*

Cancer Liaison Program (CLP)
Food and Drug Administration (FDA)
Room 9-49CFH-12
5600 Fishers Lane
Rockville, MD 20857
(888) INFO-FDA [463-6332]
http://www.fda.gov
*The Cancer Liaison Program is a division of the FDA and works
directly with cancer patients and advocacy programs to
provide information and education on the FDA drug-approval
process, cancer clinical trials, and access to investigational
therapies when entering into an existing clinical trial is not
possible.*

National Cancer Institute (NCI)
Building 31, Room 10A03
31 Center Drive, MSC 2580
Bethesda, MD 20892-2580
(301) 435-3848
(800) 422-6237
http://www.cancer.gov
*The NCI provides accurate, up-to-date information on many types
of cancer, information on clinical trials, resources for people
dealing with cancer, and information for researchers and
health professionals. Help is also available for the deaf and in
Spanish.*

National Center for Complementary and Alternative Medicine
NCCAM Clearinghouse
P.O. Box 7923
Gaithersburg, MD 20893-7923
(301) 519-3153
(888) 644-6226
(866) 464-3615 (TTY)
http://www.nccam.nih.gov
*The NCCAM supports rigorous research on complementary and
alternative medicine (CAM), trains researchers in CAM, and
disseminates information to the public and professionals on which
CAM modalities work, which do not, and why. The center offers
information packages, fact sheets, a newsletter, referrals, meetings
and workshops, and treatment information.*

OncoLink
(215) 349-5445
http://www.oncolink.upenn.edu
Affiliated with the University of Pennsylvania Cancer Center, this comprehensive Web site provides information about specific types of cancer, updates on cancer treatments, and news about research advances.

Vital Options International TeleSupport Cancer Network
15821 Ventura Boulevard, Suite 645
Encino, CA 91436-2946
(818) 788-5225
(800) 477-7666
info@vitaloptions.org
http://www.vitaloptions.org
The mission of Vital Options is to use communications technology to reach people dealing with cancer. This organization holds a weekly syndicated call-in cancer radio talk show called The Group Room, *which provides a forum for patients, long-term survivors, family members, physicians, and therapists to discuss cancer issues. Listeners can participate in the show during its broadcast every Sunday from 4 P.M. to 6 P.M. Eastern time by calling the toll-free telephone number. A live Web simulcast of* The Group Room *can be heard by logging onto the Vital Options Web site.*

CANCER SURVIVORS
Cancer Survivors Network
American Cancer Society (ACS)
1599 Clifton Road NE
Atlanta, GA 30329-4251
(877) 333-4673
http://www.acscsn.org
This is a Web-based service for cancer survivors, their families, caregivers, and friends. The network provides survivors and families access to prerecorded discussions. The Web-based component offers live online chat sessions, virtual support groups, prerecorded talk shows, and personal stories.

The Young Survival Coalition
Box 528, 52A Carmine Street
New York, NY 10014
(212) 916-7667

http://www.youngsurvival.org
*Organization that focuses on the issues and challenges faced by
women aged 40 and under who are diagnosed with breast cancer.*

CAREGIVERS

National Family Caregivers Association (NFCA)
10400 Connecticut Avenue, Suite 500
Kensington, MD 20895-3944
(301) 942-6430
(800) 896-3650
http://www.nfcacares.org
*NFCA provides educational and emotional support for family
caregivers; advocacy; individual, family, group, peer, and
bereavement counseling; and information.*

CERVICAL CANCER

Center for Cervical Health
54 Sunrise Boulevard
Toms River, NJ 08753
(732) 255-1132
http://www.cervicalhealth.org
*The Center for Cervical Health is a nonprofit organization that provides
emotional support for women and their families touched by cervical
disease and also provides information to the public and professionals
on cervical health issues through education and advocacy.*

National Breast and Cervical Cancer Early Detection Program
Centers for Disease Control and Prevention
4770 Buford Highway NE, MS K64
Atlanta, GA 30341
(888) 842-6355
http://www.cdc.gov/cancer/nbccedp
*A CDC program that provides screening services, including clinical
breast examinations, mammograms, pelvic examinations, and
Pap tests, to underserved women. The program also funds post-
screening diagnostic services, such as surgical consultation and
biopsy, to ensure that all women with abnormal results receive
timely and adequate referrals. Provides breast and cervical
cancer screening; referrals; public information and education
programs; and appropriate surveillance and epidemiological
systems.*

National Cervical Cancer Coalition
16501 Sherman Way, Suite # 110
Van Nuys, CA 91406
(818) 909-3849
(800) 685-5531
http://www.nccc-online.org
A grassroots advocacy group whose goal is to educate the public
and legislators about the issues facing cervical cancer patients,
including Pap smear reimbursement, access to testing for all
women, and treatment and research in the field of cervical
cancer.

CHEMOTHERAPY

Chemocare.com
231 North Avenue
Westfield, NJ 07090
(800) 552-4366
(908) 233-1103
http://www.chemocare.com
Scott Hamilton's Web site is designed to provide the latest
information about chemotherapy to patients and their families,
caregivers, and friends.

Chemotherapy Foundation
183 Madison Avenue, Suite 302
New York NY 10016
(212) 213-9292
http://www.chemotherapyfoundation.org
Established in 1968, the Chemotherapy Foundation is dedicated to
the control, cure, and prevention of cancer through innovative lab
and clinical research, and to the special education of patients.

CHILDREN/TEENS AND CANCER

Brain Tumor Foundation for Children, Inc. (BTFC)
1835 Savoy Drive, Suite 316
Atlanta, GA 30341
(770) 458-5554
http://www.btfcgainc.org
A nonprofit organization that provides information and patient
services for children with brain tumors. Provides family support and
education programs, public awareness and information activities, a

*telephone support network, and regular meetings and recreational
events for children and their families. BTFC also funds research.*

Candlelighters Childhood Cancer Foundation (CCCF)
Post Office Box 498
Kensington, MD 20895-0498
(301) 962-3520
(800) 366-2223
info@candlelighters.org
http://www.candlelighters.org
*The CCCF is a nonprofit organization that provides information,
peer support, and advocacy for individuals affected by childhood
cancer, through publications, an information clearinghouse, and
a network of local support groups. A financial aid list is available
that lists organizations to which eligible families may apply for
assistance.*

Children's Brain Tumor Foundation (CBTF)
274 Madison Avenue, Suite 1301
New York, NY 10016
(212) 448-9494
(866) 228-4673
info@cbtf.org
http://www.cbtf.org
*The CBTF is a nonprofit organization that funds research and
provides support, education, and advocacy for children with
brain and spinal cord tumors and their families. It also provides
educational materials (including a Spanish-language publication)
and cosponsors conferences and seminars for families, survivors,
and health-care professionals that offer the latest information
about research, treatments, and strategies for living. Through
CBTF's Parent-to-Parent Network, families share their experiences
with others in similar situations.*

The Children's Cancer Association
7524 S.W. Macadam Avenue, Suite B
Portland, OR 97219
(503) 244-3141
http://www.childrenscancerassociation.org
*The Alexandra Ellis Memorial Children's Cancer Association is
dedicated to improving the care and quality of Oregon children
with cancer and life-threatening illnesses and to ease the burdens
of their families. Services include a Kids' Cart Tune hospital music*

program, Pediatric Chemo Pal Program, family resource center, Kids Cancer Pages, a Dream Catcher Wishing Program, and medical presentations.

The Children's Cause, Inc.
1010 Wayne Street, Suite 770
Silver Spring, MD 20910
(301) 562-2765
http://www.childrenscause.org
The Children's Cause is dedicated to accelerating the discovery and access to innovative, safer, and more effective treatments for childhood cancer. Services include advocacy, counseling for children with cancer and long-term survivors, training workshops, educational programs, referrals, and information on clinical trials.

Children's Hopes & Dreams Foundation Inc.
280 Route 46
Dover, NJ 07801
(973) 361-7366
http://www.childrenswishes.org
This foundation offers a pen pal program for children five through 17 (and their siblings) who have been diagnosed with a life-threatening and chronic illnesses or crisis situation. Services include housing and children's services.

Children's Hospice International
901 North Pitt Street, Suite 230
Alexandria, VA 22314
(703) 684-0330
(800) 242-4453
chiorg@aol.com
http://www.chionline.org
Children's Hospice International provides a network of support for dying children and their families. It serves as a clearinghouse for research programs and support groups and offers educational materials and training programs on pain management and the care of seriously ill children.

Children's Organ Transplant Association, Inc.
2501 COTA Drive
Bloomington, IN 47403
(812) 336-8872
(800) 366-2682

http://www.cota.org
COTA provides support and financial assistance to the families
of children who need organ transplants, educates the public
about the need for organ donors, promotes and contributes to
medical research to develop new antirejection drugs for transplant
recipients, and has built a network of COTA organizations to
coordinate services nationwide. Services include a speaker's
bureau, cancer information, and a toll-free information line.

Friends Network
P.O. Box 4545
Santa Barbara, CA 93140
http://www.cancerfunletter.com
This national nonprofit organization offers a color cancer activities
newsletter (The Funletter) *to help children with cancer.*

Kids Konnected
27071 Cabot Road, Suite 102
Laguna Hills, CA 92653
(800) 899-2866
(949) 582-5443
info@kidskonnected.org
http://www.kidskonnected.org
The original Kids Konnected was formed in 1993 as Komen Kids by
then-ll-year-old Jon Wagner-Holtz after his mother was treated
for breast cancer. At that time there were no programs where Jon
could talk to other kids who knew what it was like to have a
sick parent, so Jon decided to change things by starting his own
hotline to help other kids going through similar situations. Today
Kids Konnected provides friendship, education, and support to
kids who have a parent with cancer.

Locks of Love
2925 10th Avenue North, Suite 102
Lake Worth, FL 33461
(561) 963-1677
(888) 896-1588
http://www.locksoflove.org
Locks of Love is a nonprofit organization that provides hairpieces to
financially disadvantaged children under age 18 across the United
States who are suffering from hair loss. The group provides hair
prosthetics, resources, volunteer services, and a newsletter. Locks
of Love accepts donations of human hair; donations must be 10

inches or longer, clean and dry, bundled in a ponytail or braid, and not too gray.

National Childhood Cancer Foundation (NCCF)
440 East Huntington Drive
P.O. Box 60012
Arcadia, CA 91066-6012
(626) 447-1674
(800) 458-6223
info@nccf.org
http://www.nccf.org

The NCCF supports research conducted by a network of institutions, each of which has a team of doctors, scientists, and other specialists with the special skills required for the diagnosis, treatment, supportive care, and research on the cancers of infants, children, and young adults. Advocating for children with cancer and the centers that treat them is also a focus of the NCCF. A limited selection of Spanish-language publications is available.

National Children's Cancer Society
1015 Locust Street, Suite 600
St. Louis, MO 63101
(800) 532-6459
http://www.children-cancer.com

The mission of The National Children's Cancer Society is to improve the quality of life for children with cancer by promoting children's health through financial and in-kind assistance, advocacy, support services, and education.

National Children's Leukemia Foundation (NCLF)
172 Madison Avenue
New York, NY 10016
(212) 686-2722
(800) GIVE-HOPE [448-3467]
http://www.leukemiafoundation.org

One of the leading nonprofit organizations in the fight against leukemia and cancer for children and adults, the NCLF supports various programs to provide the cure for children and adults, and to ease the family's burden during their hospital stay. The 24-hour hotline offers comprehensive information to any caller and provides referrals for initial testing, physicians, hospital admissions, and treatment options.

Planet Cancer
1804 East 39th Street
Austin, TX 78722
(512) 481-9010
http://www.planetcancer.org
Planet Cancer is a community of young adults between 18 and 35 with cancer who support each other in communities online and face-to-face. It's a Web site to share insights and explore fears. Services include a peer-support "Planet Cancer Forum," where patients communicate directly with each other, advocacy, and "Adventure Therapy" (a type of outdoor expedition for young adults).

Ronald McDonald House
One Kroc Drive
Oak Brook, IL 60523
(630) 823-7048
http://www.rmhc.com
RMH is a national network of temporary housing facilities for families of children hospitalized with life-threatening illnesses. Many states and major cities have "Ronald McDonald Houses." Call for locations, service information, and eligibility. Services include housing, referrals, children's services, and "Family Rooms" within hospitals.

STARBRIGHT Foundation
11835 West Olympic Boulevard, Suite 500
Los Angeles, CA 90064
(310) 479-1212
(800) 315-2580
http://www.starbright.org
The STARBRIGHT Foundation creates projects that are designed to help seriously ill children and adolescents cope with the psychosocial and medical challenges they face. The STARBRIGHT Foundation produces materials such as interactive educational CD-ROMs and videos about medical conditions and procedures, advice on talking with a health professional, and other issues related to children and adolescents who have serious medical conditions. All materials are available to children, adolescents, and their families free of charge. Staff can respond to calls in Spanish.

The Ulman Cancer Fund for Young Adults
5575 Sterrett Place, Suite 340A
Columbia, MD 21044

(410) 964-0202
(888) 393-3863
info@ulmanfund.org
http://www.ulmanfund.org
*Since 1997, the fund has been working to provide young adults and
their families with a unique and comprehensive system of support.
Its mission is to provide support programs, education, and
resources, free of charge, to benefit young adults, their families
and friends who are affected by cancer and to promote awareness
and prevention of cancer. Serves young adults worldwide through
its Web site and support groups for young adults affected by
cancer and their families and friends.*

CLINICAL TRIALS
Cancer Liaison Program (CLP)
Food and Drug Administration (FDA Room 9-49CFH-12)
5600 Fishers Lane
Rockville, MD 20857
(888) INFO-FDA [463-6332]
http://www.fda.gov
*As a division of the FDA, the Cancer Liaison Program works directly
with cancer patients and advocacy programs. They provide
information and education on the FDA drug-approval process,
cancer clinical trials, and access to investigational therapies when
entering into an existing clinical trial is not possible.*

Coalition of National Cancer Cooperative Groups, Inc.
1818 Market Street, #1100
Philadelphia, PA 19103
(877) 520-4457
http://www.cancertrialshelp.org
*The Coalition of National Cancer Cooperative Groups, Inc., is the
nation's premier network of cancer clinical trials specialists.
The coalition offers a variety of programs and information,
for physicians, payers, patient advocate groups, and patients,
designed to improve the clinical trials process. The site provides
basic information about cancer clinical trials, a list of available
trials offered by seven cooperative groups, and helpful links to
patient advocate groups.*

National Cancer Institute: Clinical Trials at NIH
(888) NCI-1937
ncicssc@mail.nih.gov

http://ccr.cancer.gov/trials/cssc/
This Web site offers in-depth information on clinical trials.

COLORECTAL CANCER

Colon Cancer Alliance (CCA)
175 Ninth Avenue
New York, NY 10011
(212) 627-7451 (main office)
(877) 422-2030 (Helpline)
info@ccalliance.org
http://www.ccalliance.org
The CCA is an organization of colon and rectal cancer survivors,
their families, caregivers, and the medical community. The
alliance provides patient support and public education, supports
research, and advocates for the needs of cancer patients and their
families. The CCA offers information including brochures and
booklets, a newsletter, a toll-free helpline, and weekly online chats.
It also offers the CCA Buddies Network, which matches survivors
and caregivers with others in a similar situation for one-on-one
emotional support. The CCA has volunteers who speak Spanish.

Colorectal Cancer Network
P.O. Box 182
Kensington, MD 20895-0182
(301) 879-1500
ccnetwork@colorectal-cancer.net
http://www.colorectal-cancer.net
The Colorectal Cancer Network is a national advocacy group that
raises public awareness about colorectal cancer and provides
support services to colorectal cancer patients and their families,
friends, and caregivers. Services include support groups; an
Internet chat room; e-mail listservs for survivors, caregivers, and
advocates; hospital visitation programs; and a "One on One"
service that connects newly diagnosed individuals with long-
term survivors. The network also provides literature on screening,
diagnosis, treatment, and supportive care for colorectal cancer.

National Colorectal Cancer Research Alliance (NCCRA)
(800) 872-3000
http://www.nccra.org
Cofounded by Katie Couric and Lily Tartikoff, the NCCRA is
dedicated to the eradication of colon cancer by harnessing the

power of celebrity to promote education, fund-raising, research, and early medical screening. The site offers information on screening tests, a health checklist, a fact sheet, and information on clinical research.

United Ostomy Association, Inc.
19772 MacArthur Boulevard, Suite 200
Irvine, CA 92612-2405
(949) 660-8624
(800) 826-0826 (6:30 A.M.–4:30 P.M., Pacific time)
uoa@deltanet.com
http://www.uoa.org
The United Ostomy Association helps ostomy patients through mutual aid and emotional support. It provides information to patients and the public and sends volunteers to visit with new ostomy patients. Call for a listing of local chapters. Services include publications, OQ (quarterly newsletter), peer groups, and educational material.

COPING
CancerCare, Inc.
275 Seventh Avenue
New York, NY 10001
(212) 712-8400
(800) 813-HOPE [4673]
info@cancercare.org
http://www.cancercare.org
A national nonprofit agency that offers free support, information, and practical help to people with cancer and their loved ones. Services are available in person, over the phone, and through the agency's Web site. Spanish language help available.

CancerCare Connection (CCC)
3 Innovation Way, Suite 210
Newark, DE 19711
(302) 266-8050
(866) 266-7008
http://www.cancercareconnection.org
A nonprofit agency that provides information, referrals, and compassionate listening to people affected by cancer through a free phone service. CCC specializes in providing referrals for

services ranging from local solutions to global cancer information via a specially designed searchable database. CCC also provides referrals to physician locator services and to clinical trial principal investigators. Services offered in Delaware, southern Pennsylvania, southern New Jersey, and northern Maryland.

Cancer Hope Network
Two North Road
Chester, NJ 07930
(877) 467-3638
info@cancerhopenetwork.org
http://www.cancerhopenetwork.org
The Cancer Hope Network provides individual support to cancer patients and their families by matching them with trained volunteers who have undergone and recovered from a similar cancer experience. Such matches are based on the type and stage of cancer, treatments used, side effects experienced, and other factors.

Cancervive, Inc.
11636 Chayote Street, Suite 500
Los Angeles, CA 90049
(310) 203-9232; (800) 4-TO-CURE
cancervive@aol.com
http://www.cancervive.org
Cancervive provides counseling, education, and advocacy to cancer patients, family members, and health professionals. The organization's patient education materials (books, documentary videos, and games) are used in every major cancer center.

CarePages
(773) 348-0720
support@carepages.com
http://www.carepages.com
CarePages are free, easy-to-use patient Web sites that help family and friends communicate when a loved one is receiving care. They can help loved ones deliver emotional support to patients and families by making it easy for them to stay in touch during a hospital stay or any time when caregiving is needed. It takes just a few minutes to create a CarePage, share it with friends and family, and build a community of support. CarePages help families create a virtual meeting place on the Web, share news and photos as often as needed, and receive emotional support during a time of need.

The Center for Attitudinal Healing
33 Buchanan Drive
Sausalito, CA 94965
(415) 331-6161
http://www.healingcenter.org
CAH is an agency providing nonsectarian spiritual and emotional support.

Comfort Connection
269 East Main Street
Newark, DE 19711
(302) 455-1501
The Comfort Connection is committed to improving overall well-being and making life a little more peaceful through new services aimed at supporting the mind, body, and soul. Services include massage therapy, relaxation for stress management (including muscle relaxation, guided imagery, meditation, and problem-solving tactics), counseling, nutrition support, cosmetic services, and volunteer services. Gift certificates are available.

ENCOREPlus
YWCA of the USA
Office of Women's Health Advocacy
1015 18th Street NW, Suite 700
Washington, DC 20036
(202) 467-0801
(800) 953-7587
cgould@ywca.org
http://www.ywca.org
ENCOREPlus is the YWCA's discussion and exercise program for women who have had breast cancer surgery. It is designed to help restore physical strength and emotional well-being. Any local branch of the YWCA, listed in the directory, can provide more information about ENCOREPlus.

Exceptional Cancer Patient, Inc. (EcaP)
522 Jackson Park Drive
Meadville, PA 16335
(814) 337-8192
http://www.ecap-online.org

*EcaP offers programs and services to cancer patients, people with
terminal illness, and health professionals. Services are based in
Connecticut only; referrals national.*

Gilda's Club Worldwide
322 Eighth Avenue, Suite 1402
New York, NY 10001
(888) 445-3248
info@gildasclub.org
http://www.gildasclub.org
*Gilda's Club Worldwide works with communities to start and
maintain local Gilda's Clubs, which provide social and emotional
support to cancer patients, their families, and friends. In addition,
it is a leading global advocate for the principle that emotional and
social support are as essential as medical care when cancer is in
the family. Lectures, workshops, support and networking groups,
special events, and children's programs are offered. Services are
available in Spanish.*

The Group Room Radio Talk Show
Vital Options TeleSupport Cancer Network
15821 Ventura Boulevard, Suite 645
Encino, CA 91436
(818) 788-5225
(800) GRP-ROOM
http://www.vitaloptions.org
*A weekly syndicated call-in cancer talk show linking patients, survivors,
and health-care professionals. Call for a station in your area. Services
include how to use communication technology, counseling and
support for patients and their families and friends, and referrals.*

I Can Cope
American Cancer Society (ACS)
1599 Clifton Road NE
Atlanta, GA 30329-4251
(800) 227-2345
http://www.cancer.org/docroot/ESN/content/ESN_3_1X_I_Can_
Cope.asp
*I Can Cope is an educational program for people facing cancer—
either personally or as a friend or family caregiver. Living with
cancer can be one of the greatest challenges a person can face
in the course of a lifetime. I Can Cope offers help in the form of*

reliable information, peer support, and practical coping skills, so that you can meet this challenge. I Can Cope classes are taught by doctors, nurses, social workers, and other health-care professional or community representatives. The sessions help dispel cancer myths by presenting straightforward facts and answers to your cancer-related questions.

Look Good . . . Feel Better
CTFA Foundation
1101 17th Street NW
Washington, DC 20036
(800) 395-5665
(202) 331-1770
http://www.lookgoodfeelbetter.org
This program was developed by the Cosmetic, Toiletry, and Fragrance Association Foundation in cooperation with American Cancer Society and the National Cosmetology Association. It focuses on techniques that can help people undergoing cancer treatment improve their appearance. The entire program is also available in Spanish.

Make Today Count
1235 East Cherokee Street
Springfield, MO 65804
(800) 432-2273
Founded in 1974, Make Today Count (MTC) provides self-help support groups in nearly 200 communities throughout the United States for patients with cancer and other life-threatening illness, their families, and the professionals who work with them. MTC is a nonprofit organization supported by individual contributions, newsletter subscriptions, and gifts. Monthly meetings are provided by each chapter, where members are encouraged to share their experiences in living with life-threatening illness. MTC publishes its founder's books and Make Today Count *(newsletter) bimonthly—organizational news, accounts of personal experiences with cancer or other life-threatening illness, and suggested readings on related topics.*

National Coalition for Cancer Survivorship (NCCS)
(877) 622-7937
http://www.canceradvocacy.org
NCCS is a network of groups and individuals that offers support to cancer survivors and their loved ones. It provides information and resources on cancer support advocacy and quality-of-life

*issues. A section of the NCCS Web site and a limited selection of
publications are available in Spanish.*

Patient Advocate Foundation (PAF)
700 Thimble Shoals Boulevard, Suite 200
Newport News, VA 23606
(757) 873-6668
(800) 532-5274
help@patientadvocate.org
http://www.patientadvocate.org
*A national network for health-care work, which also provides
education, legal counseling, and referrals to cancer patients and
survivors concerning managed care, insurance, financial issues,
job discrimination, and debt crisis matters. The Patient Assistance
Program is a subsidiary of the PAF and provides financial
assistance to patients who meet certain qualifications.*

R. A. Bloch Cancer Foundation, Inc.
4400 Main Street
Kansas City, MO 64111
(800) 433-0464
http://www.blochcancer.org
*The R. A. Bloch Cancer Foundation matches newly diagnosed
cancer patients with trained, home-based volunteers who have
been treated for the same type of cancer. They also distribute
informational materials, including a multidisciplinary list of
institutions that offer second opinions. Information is available in
Spanish.*

Vital Options International TeleSupport Cancer Network
(800) 477-7666
info@vitaloptions.org
http://www.vitaloptions.org
*An organization that facilitates a weekly syndicated call-in cancer
talk show linking callers with other patients, long-term survivors,
family members, physicians, researchers, and therapists. Offers
services in English and French.*

The Wellness Community
35 East 7th Street, Suite 412
Cincinnati, OH 45202
(513) 421-7111

(888) 793-9355
help@wellness-community.org
http://www.thewellnesscommunity.org/
The Wellness Community provides free psychological and emotional
support to cancer patients and their families. They offer support
groups on stress reduction and cancer education workshops,
nutrition guidance, exercise sessions, and social events.

FINANCIAL HELP
Air Care Alliance
1515 East 71st Street, Suite 312
Tulsa, OK 74136
(918) 745-0384
(888) 260-9707
http://www.aircareall.org
The Air Care Alliance is a nationwide league of humanitarian
flying organizations dedicated to community service. The ACA
has member groups whose activities involve health care, patient
transport, and related kinds of public benefit flying.

AIRLIFELINE
50 Fullerton Court, Suite 200
Sacramento, CA 95825
(916) 641-7800
(877) AIRLIFE
http://www.airlifeline.org
Airlifeline provides transportation to and from medical destinations
for patients in financial need. The group will fly 1,000 air miles
from any departure point in the United States.

American Kidney Fund (AKF)
6110 Executive Boulevard, Suite 1010
Rockville, MD 20852
(301) 881-3052
(800) 638-8299
http://www.kidneyfund.org
A national voluntary health organization dedicated to relieving the
staggering financial burden associated with chronic kidney failure
through patient aid programs and by offering direct financial
assistance.

The Bone Marrow Foundation
70 East 55th Street, 20th Floor
New York, NY 10022

(212) 838-3029
(800) 365-1336
http://www.bonemarrow.org
Provides eligible transplant candidates with financial assistance limited to help defray the cost of ancillary services needed to ensure proper care during the transplant procedure, as well as in pre- and post-transplant treatment phases.

CancerCare, Inc.
(800) 813-HOPE [813-4673]
info@cancercare.org
http://www.cancercare.org
A national nonprofit agency that offers free financial assistance and practical help to people with cancer and their loved ones. Services are available in person, over the phone, and through the agency's Web site. Spanish language help available.

Cancer Fund of America
2901 Breezewood Lane
Knoxville, TN 37921-1009
(865) 938-5281
http://www.cfoa.org
CFA is dedicated to providing direct aid to financially indigent patients in the form of goods.

Corporate Angel Network, Inc. (CAN)
Westchester County Airport, Building 1
White Plains, NY 10604
(914) 328-1313
(866) 328-1313
info@corpangelnetwork.org
http://www.corpangelnetwork.org
CAN finds free air transportation (on corporate planes) for cancer patients who need medical treatment. Patients must be ambulatory.

Ensure Health Connection
P.O. Box 29139
Shawnee, KS 66201
(800) 986-8501
http://www.ensure.com
Provides coupons and valuable information to people in need of the nutritional supplement Ensure. Ensure donates their product to food banks, where a person in need may be able to receive a free supply when available.

Hill-Burton Free Hospital Care
5600 Fishers Lane
Rockville, MD 20857
(800) 638-0742
(301) 443-5656
dfcrcomm@hrsa.gov
http://www.hrsa.gov/osp/dfcr/
*Hill-Burton is a program run by the U.S. government that can
arrange for certain medical facilities or hospitals to provide free or
low-cost care. For information, call the hotline or access through
their Web site (click on "Obtaining Free Care").*

The Medicine Program
P.O. Box 520
Doniphan, AL 63935
(573) 996-7300
http://www.themedicineprogram.com
*Provides free prescription medicine to those who qualify. Services
include assistance for medicine. The Medicine Program requires a
$5 processing fee for each medication requested.*

Mission of Hope Cancer Fund
802 First Street
Jackson, MI 49023
(517) 782-4643
(888) 544-6423
http://www.cancerfund.org
*A nonprofit organization established by a cancer survivor to help
cancer patients and their families with special financial needs. Their
goal is to help relieve some of the extra financial burdens of cancer
patients and their families while dealing with cancer treatment
and recovery. Services include information education, counseling,
housing, financial assistance, and assistance for medications.*

National Association of Hospital Hospitality
4915 Auburn Avenue
Bethesda, MD 20814
(800) 542-9730
http://comnet.org
*A nonprofit corporation serving facilities that provide lodging and
other supportive services to patients and their families when
confronted with medical emergencies. Services include referrals
and housing/lodging facilities.*

National Patient Air Transport Hotline
P.O. Box 1940
Manassas, VA 22110-0804
(800) 296-1217
http://www.npath.org
*NPATH is a clearinghouse for patients who cannot afford travel for
medical care.*

National Patient Travel Center (NPTC)
4620 Haygood Road, Suite One
Virginia Beach, VA 23455
(800) 296-1217
mercymedical@erols.com
http://www.patienttravel.org
*The NPTC provides the National Patient Travel Helpline, a service
which facilitates patient access to charitable medical air
transportation resources in the United States. The NPTC also offers
information about discounted airline ticket programs for patients
and patient escorts, operates Special-Lift and Child-Lift programs,
and brings ambulatory outpatients to the United States from many
overseas locations.*

Patient Advocate Foundation (PAF)
700 Thimble Shoals Boulevard, Suite 200
Newport News, VA 23606
(757) 873-6668
(800) 532-5274
help@patientadvocate.org
http://www.patientadvocate.org
*The PAF provides financial assistance to those who meet certain
qualifications, as well as education, legal counseling, and referrals
to cancer patients and survivors concerning managed care,
insurance, financial issues, job discrimination, and debt crisis
matters. The Patient Assistance Program is a subsidiary of the PAF.*

Ronald McDonald House Charities
One Kroc Drive
Oak Brook, IL 60523
(630) 623-7048
http://www.rmhc.com
*RMH is a national network of temporary housing facilities for
families of children hospitalized with life-threatening illnesses.
Many states and major cities have "Ronald McDonald Houses."*

Call for locations, service information, and eligibility. Services include housing/lodging, referrals, and children's services.

GASTROINTESTINAL STROMAL TUMOR (GIST)
The Life Raft Group
(973) 837-9092
pbarckett@liferaftgroup.org
http://www.liferaftgroup.org/
The Life Raft Group is a nonprofit organization providing support through information, education, and innovative research to patients with a rare cancer called GIST (gastrointestinal stromal tumor). Their outreach efforts touch patients and their doctors throughout the world.

HOSPICE
Children's Hospice International
901 North Pitt Street, Suite 230
Alexandria, VA 22314
(703) 684-0330
(800) 242-4453
chiorg@aol.com
http://www.chionline.org
Children's Hospice International provides a network of support for dying children and their families. It serves as a clearinghouse for research programs and support groups and offers educational materials and training programs on pain management and the care of seriously ill children.

Hospice Education Institute
3 Unity Square
P.O. Box 98
Machiasport, ME 04655-0098
(207) 255-8800
(800) 331-1620
http://www.hospiceworld.org
An independent, nonprofit organization that offers information and education about the many facets of caring for the dying and the bereaved. It offers a toll-free information and the referral service, HospiceLink (see below), which helps patients and their families find support services in their communities, along with regional seminars, professional education, advice, and assistance. The

group can refer cancer patients and their families to local hospice and palliative care programs.

HOSPICELINK
Three Unity Square
P.O. Box 98
Machiasport, ME 04655-0098
(207) 255-8800
(800) 331-1620
HOSPICEALL@aol.com
http://www.hospiceworld.org
HOSPICELINK helps patients and their families find support services in their communities. They offer information about hospice and palliative care and can refer cancer patients and their families to local hospice and palliative care programs.

National Hospice and Palliative Care Organization (NHPCO)
1700 Diagonal Road, Suite 625
Alexandria, VA 22314
(703) 837-1500
(800) 658-8898
info@nhpco.org
http://www.nhpco.org
The NHPCO is an association of programs that provide hospice and palliative care. It is designed to increase awareness about hospice services and to champion the rights and issues of terminally ill patients and their family members. They offer discussion groups, publications, information about how to find a hospice and information about the financial aspects of hospice. Some Spanish-language publications are available, and staff are able to answer calls in Spanish.

KIDNEY CANCER
American Association of Kidney Patients
3505 East Frontage Road, Suite 315
Tampa, FL 33607
(800) 749-2257
http://www.aakp.org

American Foundation for Urologic Disease (AFUD)
1120 North Charles Street
Baltimore, MD 21201

(410) 468-1800
(800) 242-2383
http://www.afud.org

The mission of the American Foundation for Urologic Disease is the prevention and cure of urologic disease, through the expansion of patient education, public awareness, research, and advocacy. Provides support groups for people with prostate cancer. Services include a toll-free phone line, a resource guide on prostate cancer, support group listings, and referrals for incontinence and erectile dysfunctions. There is also a Spanish-speaking operator.

American Kidney Fund (AKF)
6110 Executive Boulevard, Suite 1010
Rockville, MD 20852
(301) 881-3052
(800) 638-8299
http://www.kidneyfund.org

A national voluntary health organization dedicated to improving the daily lives of people with chronic kidney disease. The AKF's primary goal is to relieve the often staggering financial burden associated with chronic kidney failure through patient aid programs by offering direct financial assistance.

Kidney Cancer Association
1234 Sherman Avenue, Suite 203
Evanston, IL 60202-1375
(847) 332-1051
(800) 850-9132
office@kidneycancerassociation.org
http://www.kidneycancerassociation.org

The Kidney Cancer Association supports research, offers printed materials about the diagnosis and treatment of kidney cancer, sponsors support groups, and provides physician referral information.

National Kidney and Urologic Diseases Information Clearinghouse
3 Information Way
Bethesda, MD 20892
(301) 654-4415
http://kidney.niddk.nih.gov

National Kidney Foundation
30 East 33rd Street
New York, NY 10016

(800) 622-9010
http://www.kidney.org

LESBIAN/GAY ISSUES
The Mautner Project for Lesbians with Cancer
(202) 332-5536
mautner@mautnerproject.org
http://www.mautnerproject.org
*Provides support, education, information, and advocacy for health
  issues relating to lesbians with cancer and their families. Help also
  available in Spanish.*

LEUKEMIA
The Leukemia and Lymphoma Society
1311 Mamaroneck Avenue
White Plains, NY 10605-5221
(914) 949-5213
(800) 955-4572
infocenter@leukemia-lymphoma.org
http://www.leukemia-lymphoma.org
*The goal of the society is to find cures for leukemia, lymphoma,
  Hodgkin's disease, and multiple myeloma and to improve the quality
  of life of patients and their families. The society provides patient
  financial aid for specified treatment expenses and transportation,
  family support groups, First Connection (a professionally supervised
  peer support program), referrals, and school reentry materials. Help
  is also available in Spanish, French, Portuguese, and Japanese.*

Leukemia Society of America
733 Third Avenue
New York, NY 10017
(800) 955-4572
(812) 573-8484
http://www.leukemia.org
*The world's largest organization dedicated to funding research,
  services, and education.*

National Children's Leukemia Foundation
172 Madison Avenue
New York, NY 10016
(212) 686-2722

(800) GIVE-HOPE [448-3467]
http://www.leukemiafoundation.org
One of the leading nonprofit organizations in the fight against leukemia and cancer for children and adults. The NCLF is established to support the unfortunate in various programs, to provide the cure for children and adults, and to ease the family's burden during their hospital stay. The 24-hour hotline, (800) GIVE-HOPE, offers comprehensive information to any caller and provides referrals for initial testing, physicians, hospital admissions, and treatment options.

LIVER CANCER
About Liver Tumors
(502) 629-3380
info@AboutLiverTumors.com
http://www.aboutlivertumors.com
A resource for liver patients and concerned persons. This Web site is an excellent resource that includes frequently asked questions, definitions, as well as a portal for people to contact physicians and support groups.

American Liver Foundation
75 Maiden Lane, Suite 603
New York, NY 10038
(800) GO-LIVER
info@liverfoundation.org
http://www.liverfoundation.org
A national voluntary nonprofit organization dedicated to the prevention, treatment, and cure of hepatitis and other liver diseases through research, education, and legal or patient advocacy assistance. Services include referrals, a newsletter, providing guest speakers, and advocacy. The foundation also provides funding for research and educational programs.

LUNG CANCER
Alliance for Lung Cancer Advocacy, Support, and Education (ALCASE)
P.O. Box 849
Vancouver, WA 98666
(360) 696-2436
(800) 298-2436

info@alcase.org
http://www.alcase.org
*ALCASE offers programs designed to help improve the quality of life
of people with lung cancer and their families. Programs include
education about the disease, psychosocial support, and advocacy
about issues that concern lung cancer survivors.*

American Lung Association
61 Broadway, 6th Floor
New York, NY 10006
(212) 315-8700
(800) LUNG-USA
info@lungusa.org
http://www.lungusa.org
*ALA is a national nonprofit organization dedicated to conquering
lung disease and promoting lung health. Services include
cancer information, professional education, smoking cessation
programs, and a speakers bureau. Services are available in
Spanish.*

Lung Cancer.org
http://www.lungcancer.org
*An educational group offering information about lung cancer to the
community.*

LYMPHEDEMA
National Lymphedema Network, Inc.
1611 Telegraph Avenue, Suite 1111
Oakland, CA 94612-2138
(510) 208-3200
(800) 541-3259
nln@lymphnet.org
http://www.lymphnet.org
*The NLN provides education and guidance to lymphedema patients,
health-care professionals, and the general public by disseminating
information on the prevention and management of primary and
secondary lymphedema. They provide a toll-free support hotline, a
referral service to lymphedema treatment centers and health-care
professionals, a quarterly newsletter with information about medical
and scientific developments, support groups, pen pals, educational
courses for health-care professionals and patients, and a computer
database. Some Spanish-language materials are available.*

LYMPHOMA
Cure for Lymphoma Foundation
215 Lexington Avenue
New York, NY 10016
(212) 213-9595
(800) CFL-6848
http://www.cfl.org
A nonprofit organization established to raise money for lymphoma
research, support, and education for those whose lives have been
touched by lymphoma.

Cutaneous Lymphoma Network
c/o Department of Dermatology
234 Goodman Street
Cincinnati, OH 45267-0523
http://www.med.uc.edu/departme/dermatol/dermatol.htm
Provides a newsletter distributed quarterly to 1,800 physicians and
patients. Working on producing a videotape to educate about the
disease and treatment.

The Leukemia and Lymphoma Society
1311 Mamaroneck Avenue
White Plains, NY 10605
(914) 949-5213
(800) 955-4572
http://www.leukemia-lymphoma.org
The goal of the society is to find cures for leukemia, lymphoma,
Hodgkin's disease, and multiple myeloma and to improve the quality
of life of patients and their families. The society provides patient
financial aid for specified treatment expenses and transportation,
family support groups, First Connection (a professionally supervised
peer support program), referrals, and school reentry materials. Help
is also available in Spanish, French, Portuguese, and Japanese.

Lymphoma Foundation of America
P.O. Box 15335
Chevy Chase, MD 20825
(202) 223-6181
Lymphoma Foundation of America is a nonprofit charitable
organization devoted to helping lymphoma patients and their
families.

Lymphoma Research Foundation (LRF)
8800 Venice Boulevard, Suite 207
Los Angeles, CA 90034
(310) 204-7040
(800) 500-9976
LRF@lymphoma.org (general information)
helpline@lymphoma.org (patient services)
http://www.lymphoma.org
In 2001, the Lymphoma Research Foundation of America (LRFA) and the Cure for Lymphoma Foundation (CFL) merged to become the Lymphoma Research Foundation (LRF). The LRF's mission is to eradicate lymphoma and serve those touched by this disease. The LRF funds research, advocates for lymphoma-related legislation, and provides educational and support programs for patients and their families. LRFA offers a helpline for general information on lymphoma, as well as referrals to the resources, oncologists, clinical trials, and support groups. A buddy program is available to match newly diagnosed patients with other lymphoma patients who have coped with the disease.

MESOTHELIOMA
Life with Mesothelioma
(800) 780-2686
http://www.lifewithmesothelioma.com

Mesothelioma Information and Resource Group
(888) 802-6376
info@mirg.org
http://www.mirg.org/
The Mesothelioma Information and Resource Group (MIRG) is an organization created to assist patients, family, friends, and loved ones in learning about mesothelioma and other asbestos-related injuries. It is the aim of MIRG to provide information about the disease, its causes, its treatment, and its personal and legal impact.

MINORITIES AND CANCER
National Asian Women's Health Organization (NAWHO)
250 Montgomery Street, Suite 900

San Francisco, CA 94104
(415) 989-9747
nawho@nawho.org
http://www.nawho.org
*The NAWHO is working to improve the health status of Asian women
and families through research, education, leadership, and public
policy programs. They have resources for Asian women in English,
Cantonese, Laotian, Vietnamese, and Korean. Publications on
subjects such as reproductive rights, breast and cervical cancer,
and tobacco control are available.*

National Latina Health Organization
P.O. Box 7567
Oakland, CA 94601
(510) 534-1362
*An organization committed to establishing bilingual access to quality
health care and self-empowerment of Latinas, through health
education, health advocacy, and public policy. All Latinas as well
as women of color are welcome.*

Sisters Network, Inc.
8787 Woodway Drive, Suite 4206
Houston, TX 77063
(866) 781-1808
sisnet4@aol.com
http://www.sistersnetworkinc.org
*Sisters Network seeks to increase local and national attention
to the impact that breast cancer has in the African-American
community. All chapters are run by breast cancer survivors
and receive volunteer assistance from community leaders and
associate members. The services provided by Sisters Network
include individual/group support, community education,
advocacy, and research. The national headquarters serves as
a resource and referral base for survivors, clinical trials, and
private/government agencies. Teleconferences are held to update
chapters with the latest information and share new ideas.
An educational brochure designed for underserved women is
available. In addition, a national African-American breast
cancer survivors newsletter is distributed to survivors, medical
facilities, government agencies, organizations, and churches
nationwide.*

MOUTH CANCER (See ORAL CANCER)

MYELOMA
International Myeloma Foundation (IMF)
12650 Riverside Drive, Suite 206
North Hollywood, CA 91607-3421
(818) 487-7455
(800) 452-2873
TheIMF@myeloma.org
http://www.myeloma.org
The IMF supports education, treatment, and research for multiple
myeloma. They provide a toll-free hotline, seminars, and
educational materials for patients and their families. Although the
IMF does not sponsor support groups, they do keep a list of other
organizations' support groups and provide information on how
to start a support group. A section of the IMF Web site and some
printed materials are available in Spanish.

The Multiple Myeloma Research Foundation (MMRF)
51 Locust Avenue, Suite 201
New Canaan, CT 06840
(203) 972-1250
info@themmrf.org
http://www.multiplemyeloma.org
The MMRF supports research grants and professional and patient
symposia on multiple myeloma and related blood cancers. The
MMRF publishes a quarterly newsletter and provides referrals and
information packets free of charge to patients and family members.

ORAL, HEAD, AND NECK CANCERS
International Association of Laryngectomees (IAL)
(866) 425-3678
IAL@larynxlink.com
http://www.larynxlink.com
An association of over 230 laryngectomee clubs. Clubs provide
pre- and post-operation visits to laryngee cancer patients and
continuing support education for laryngectomees and families.

Mouth Cancer Foundation
info@mouthcancerfoundation.org
http://www.mouthcancerfoundation.org

A not-for-profit Internet portal that aims to help patients and health professionals find free information on mouth, head, and neck cancers easily. It provides direct links to the relevant sections of existing cancer Web sites and includes patient stories as well as an active message board, which acts as an easily accessible online support group. The Web site includes firsthand patient accounts of their experiences, has sections on Treatment, Complications, Cheerful Help, Spiritual Help, HPV Risks, Tobacco Risks, etc.

National Oral Health Information Clearinghouse (NOHIC)
1 NOHIC Way
Bethesda, MD 20892-3500
(301) 402-7364
http://www.aerie.com/nohicweb/
NOHIC, a service of the National Institute of Dental and Craniofacial Research, is one of the National Institutes of Health. It provides information for both patients and professionals regarding special care topics in oral health, including oral complications of cancer treatments.

The Oral Cancer Foundation
3419 Via Lido, #205
Newport Beach, CA 92663
(949) 646-8000
info@oralcancerfoundation.org
http://www.oralcancerfoundation.org
The Oral Cancer Foundation is a nonprofit organization that is dedicated to saving lives through education, research, prevention, advocacy, and support for persons with oral cancer. The foundation provides an online Oral Cancer Forum, which includes a message board and chat room that connect newly diagnosed patients, family members, and the public.

Support for People with Oral and Head and Neck Cancers, Inc. (SPOHNC)
P.O. Box 53
Locust Valley, NY 11560-0053
(800) 377-0928
info@spohnc.org
http://www.spohnc.org
The SPOHNC is a self-help organization that serves oral and head and neck cancer patients, survivors, and their families.

*The organization offers support group meetings, information,
newsletters, and teleconferences. The SPOHNC also offers a
"Survivor to Survivor" network, which pairs survivors or their
family members with volunteers who have had a similar diagnosis
and treatment program.*

ORGAN TRANSPLANTS
Children's Organ Transplant Association, Inc.
2501 COTA Drive
Bloomington, IN 47403
(812) 336-8872
(800) 366-2682
http://www.cota.org
*COTA provides support and financial assistance to the families
of children who need organ transplants, educates the public
about the need for organ donors, promotes and contributes to
medical research to develop new antirejection drugs for transplant
recipients, and builds a network of COTA organizations to
coordinate services nationwide. Services include a speaker's
bureau, cancer information, and a toll-free information line.*

OVARIAN CANCER
CONVERSATIONS!: The International Ovarian Cancer Connection
(806) 355-2565
http://www.ovarian-news.org
Publisher of CONVERSATIONS! The International Newsletter
for Those Fighting Ovarian Cancer, *a free monthly newsletter
providing hope, humor, support, and information about treatment
options and coping tips. Survivor-to-fighter matching service
available.*

Gilda Radner Familial Ovarian Cancer Registry
Roswell Park Cancer Institute
Elm and Carlton Streets
Buffalo, NY 14263
(800) 682-7426
(716) 845-3110
http://www.ovariancancer.com
*A project collecting data on the link between heredity and ovarian
cancer. Services include genetic counseling, support groups,*

referrals, and assistance with genetic screening. (FOCR is not a treatment center.)

National Ovarian Cancer Coalition (NOCC)
500 Northeast Spanish River Boulevard, Suite 14
Boca Raton, FL 33431
(561) 393-0005
(888) 682-7426
NOCC@ovarian.org
http://www.ovarian.org
The NOCC raises awareness about ovarian cancer and promotes education about this disease. They have a toll-free number for information, referral, support, and education about ovarian cancer. They also offer support groups, a database of gynecologic oncologists searchable by state, and educational materials. A limited selection of Spanish-language publications is available.

Ovarian Cancer National Alliance (OCNA)
910 17th Street NW, Suite 413
Washington, DC 20006
(202) 331-1332
ocna@ovariancancer.org
http://www.ovariancancer.org
The alliance works to increase public and professional understanding of ovarian cancer and to advocate for research to determine more effective ways to diagnose, treat, and cure this disease. The alliance distributes informational materials; sponsors an annual advocacy conference for survivors and families; advocates on the issues of cancer to the ovarian cancer community; and works with women's groups, seniors, and health professionals to increase awareness of ovarian cancer.

The Ovarian Cancer Research Fund (OCRF)
(800) 873-9569
info@ocrf.org
http://www.ocrf.org
Dedicated to advancing research by underwriting investigations to find techniques for early detection and to aid in the development of new therapists. Raises awareness through educational outreach programs and awareness projects, including videos and resource materials.

Yale University—Ovarian Screening Program
Yale Comprehensive Cancer Center—OB/GYN
P.O. Box 208063
New Haven, CT 06520-8063
(203) 785-4014
*University offers information and screening (nationwide) to anyone at
high risk for ovarian cancer (e.g., a mother, sister, grandmother, or
aunt who has had ovarian cancer). Clinical trials are also available.
Services include referrals and genetic and diagnostic screenings.*

PAIN
American Chronic Pain Association (ACPA)
P.O. Box 850
Rocklin, CA 95677
(800) 533-3231
http://www.theacpa.org
*A self-help organization that offers educational material and peer
support to help people combat chronic pain. Provides referrals
to pain control facilities, has publications on managing daily
pain, and organizes support groups. ACPA also publishes a
quarterly newsletter and a book on coping with pain for which a
donation is requested. (It provides no direct physician referral or
biofeedback, hypnosis, or other specific services.)*

American Pain Society
4700 West Lake Avenue
Glenview, IL 60025
(847) 375-4715
http://www.ampainsoc.org
*A multidisciplinary educational and scientific organization dedicated
to serving people in pain. Members research and treat pain and
advocate for patients with pain. Services include the Pain Facilities
Directory, with information on more than 500 specialized pain
treatment centers across the country (these are usually a part or a
program of a hospital, clinic, or medical care complex), counseling
for pain, referrals, and education programs.*

National Chronic Pain Outreach Association, Inc.
P.O. Box 274
Millboro, VA 24460
(540) 862-9437
http://www.chronicpain.org

*A nonprofit organization whose purpose is to lessen the suffering
of people with chronic pain by educating pain sufferers, health-
care professionals, and the public about chronic pain and its
management.*

PANCREATIC CANCER
Hirshberg Foundation for Pancreatic Cancer
375 Homewood Road
Los Angeles, CA 90049
(310) 472-6310
agirsh@aol.com
*National nonprofit organization, supported by donations, serves as a
help-line for patients with pancreatic cancer. Primary function is
to fund research for early detection of this cancer. Services include
referrals, counseling, home care/hospice, and patient financial aid.
Two research laboratories at UCLA Medical Center are the major
recipients of the research grants.*

The Lustgarten Foundation for Pancreatic Cancer
1111 Stewart Avenue
Bethpage, NY 11714
(516) 803-2308
(516) 803-1000
lsasso@cablevision.com
http://www.lustgartenfoundation.org
*The Lustgarten Foundation funds research, advocates for research
funding, and raises awareness of pancreatic cancer diagnosis,
treatment, and prevention. The foundation assists patients
and their families in obtaining the most accurate, up-to-date
information about pancreatic cancer. It provides educational
materials and publications about pancreatic cancer, including a
Spanish-language publication. It also has an on-staff social worker
available to make referrals to cancer support services.*

National Pancreas Foundation
P.O. Box 15333
Boston, MA 02215
http://www.pancreasfoundation.org/
*Nonprofit foundation that supports research into diseases of the
pancreas and provides information and humanitarian services to
those people who are suffering from such illnesses.*

Pancreatic Cancer Action Network (PanCAN)
2221 Rosecrans Avenue, Suite 131
El Segundo, CA 90245
(310) 725-0025
(877) 272-6226
info@pancan.org
http://www.pancan.org
PanCAN, a nonprofit advocacy organization, educates health
  professionals and the general public about pancreatic cancer to
  increase awareness of the disease. PanCAN also advocates for
  increased funding of pancreatic cancer research and promotes
  access to and awareness of the latest medical advances, support
  networks, clinical trials, and reimbursement for care.

PATIENT ADVOCACY
Patient Advocate Foundation (PAF)
(800) 532-5274
help@patientadvocate.org
http://www.patientadvocate.org
The PAF provides education, legal counseling, and referrals to cancer
  patients and survivors concerning managed care, insurance,
  financial issues, job discrimination, and debt crisis matters.

PITUITARY TUMOR
Pituitary Network Association
P.O. Box 1958
Thousand Oaks, CA 91358
(805) 499-9973
http://www.pituitary.org

PROSTATE CANCER
American Foundation for Urologic Disease (AFUD)
1128 North Charles Street
Baltimore, MD 21201
(410) 468-1800
(800) 242-2383
http://www.afud.org
The AFUD supports research; provides education to patients, the
  general public, and health professionals; and offers patient support
  services for those who have or may be at risk for a urologic disease

or disorder. They provide information on urologic disease and dysfunctions, including prostate cancer treatment options, bladder health, and sexual function. They also offer prostate cancer support groups (Prostate Cancer Network). Some Spanish-language publications are available.

American Prostate Society
P.O. Box 870
Hanover, MD 21076
(800) 308-1106
ameripros@mindspring.com
http://www.ameripros.org

Man to Man
American Cancer Society
1599 Clifton Road NE
Atlanta, GA 30329
(800) 227-2345
(404) 320-3333
http://www.cancer.org
Support group that includes an educational presentation by a health-care professional. Offers support, one-on-one visitation, and telephone support from specially trained prostate cancer survivors.

Men's Cancer Resource Group
1001 South MacDill Avenue
Tampa, FL 33629
(813) 273-3652
(800) 309-6467
Organized by prostate cancer survivors and concerned professionals, the MCRG offers a support network as well as an education clearinghouse for current information on research and treatment. The group offers support group meetings and community outreach in the Tampa Bay area. Callers from anywhere can discuss concerns with another man by calling the 24-hour information line at (800) 309-6467.

National Prostate Cancer Coalition
1158 15th Street NW
Washington, DC 20005
(202) 463-9455

(888) 245-9455
info@pcacoalition.org
http://www.4npcc.org
*A grassroots advocacy organization seeking to increase prostate
cancer awareness, enhance outreach, and advocate for research
funds and better detection strategies. Services include advocacy,
public education, referrals, and information.*

Patient Advocates for Advanced Cancer Treatments (PAACT)
1143 Parmelee NW
P.O. Box 141695
Grand Rapids, MI 49504
(616) 453-1477
http://www.paactusa.org
*A nonprofit prostate cancer advocacy organization that provides
prostate cancer patients with the most advanced methods of
detection, diagnostic procedures, evaluations, and treatments. The
legal action committee can help patients with insurance problems.
Services include referrals, a public library, education information,
quarterly newsletter* Cancer Communication, *counseling, sex
therapy, advocacy, volunteer services, medical assistance,
alternative therapies, support group information, elderly services,
and health insurance information.*

Prostate Cancer Foundation
1250 Fourth Street
Santa Monica, CA 90401
(310) 570-4700
(800) 757-2873
info@prostatecancerfoundation.org
http://www.prostatecancerfoundation.org/
*The Prostate Cancer Foundation is a nonprofit organization that
provides funding for research projects to improve methods of
diagnosing and treating prostate cancer. It also offers printed
resources for prostate cancer survivors and their families. The
mission of the Prostate Cancer Foundation is to find a cure for
prostate cancer.*

US TOO! International, Inc.
5003 Fairview Avenue
Downers Grove, IL 60515-5286
(630) 795-1002

(800) 808-7866
dorothy@ustoo.com
http://www.ustoo.org
A prostate cancer support group organization. Goals of US TOO! are to educate men newly diagnosed with prostate cancer, offer support groups, and provide the latest information about treatment for this disease.

RESEARCH

American Institute for Cancer Research (AICR)
1759 R Street NW
Washington, DC 20009
(202) 328-7744
(800) 843-8114
aicrweb@aicr.org
http://www.aicr.org
AICR provides information about cancer prevention, particularly through diet and nutrition. They offer a toll-free nutrition hotline and funding of research grants. The AICR also has a wide array of consumer and health professional brochures, plus health aids about diet and nutrition and their link to cancer and cancer prevention. The AICR also offers the AICR CancerResource, an information and resource program for cancer patients. A limited selection of Spanish-language publications is available.

Cancer Research and Prevention Foundation
1600 Duke Street, Suite 500
Alexandria, VA 22314
(703) 836-4412
(800) 227-2732
info@preventcancer.org
http://www.preventcancer.org
The Cancer Research and Prevention Foundation seeks to prevent cancer by funding research and providing educational materials on early detection and nutrition.

Cancer Research Institute
681 Fifth Avenue
New York, NY 10022-4209
(212) 688-7515

(800) 99-CANCER

http://www.cancerresearch.org

A nonprofit organization that funds research projects and scientists across the country. Publishes The Cancer Research Institute Help Book *and provides information on clinical trials using immunological treatments.*

Gynecologic Cancer Foundation (GCF)

(800) 444-4441

gcf@sba.comwww.wcn.org/gcf

GCF is designed to increase public awareness of ways to prevent, detect, and treat gynecological cancers and supports innovative research.

Lance Armstrong Foundation

P.O. Box 161150

Austin, TX 78716-1150

(512) 236-8820

http://www.laf.org

The LAF, a nonprofit organization founded by cancer survivor and cyclist Lance Armstrong, provides resources and support services to people diagnosed with cancer and their families. The LAF's services include Cycle of Hope, a national cancer education campaign for people with cancer and those at risk for developing the disease, and the Cancer Profiler, a free interactive treatment decision support tool. The LAF also provides scientific and research grants for the better understanding of cancer and cancer survivorship.

National Childhood Cancer Foundation (NCCF)

440 East Huntington Drive

P.O. Box 60012

Arcadia, CA 91066-6012

(626) 447-1674

(800) 458-6223

info@nccf.org

http://www.nccf.org

The NCCF supports research conducted by a network of institutions, each of which has a team of doctors, scientists, and other specialists with the special skills required for the diagnosis, treatment, supportive care, and research on the cancers of infants, children, and young adults. Advocating for children with cancer and the centers that treat them is also a focus of the

NCCF. *A limited selection of Spanish-language publications is available.*

Susan G. Komen Breast Cancer Foundation
5005 LBJ Freeway, Suite 250
P.O. Box 650309
Dallas, TX 75244
(972) 855-1600
(800) 462-9273
http://www.komen.org
SBKCF funds research and other cancer-related programs.

SARCOMA
Sarcoma Alliance
(415) 381-7236
info@sarcomaalliance.org
http://www.sarcomaalliance.org
Strives to improve the lives of sarcoma patients through guidance, education, and support.

SKIN CANCER
About Melanoma
(502) 629-3380
info@AboutMelanoma.com
http://www.aboutmelanoma.com
A resource for melanoma patients and other concerned persons, this site is a definitive resource, providing in-depth definitions, an extensive FAQ, and a portal through which to contact physicians and experts.

The Skin Cancer Foundation
245 Fifth Avenue, Suite 1403
New York, NY 10016
(800) SKIN-490 [754-6490]
info@skincancer.org
http://www.skincancer.org
Works to increase public awareness of the importance of taking protective measures against the damaging rays of the sun and teach people how to recognize early signs of skin cancer. They conduct public and medical education programs to help reduce skin cancer.

SURVIVORS
Lance Armstrong Foundation
P.O. Box 161150

Austin, TX 78716-1150

(512) 236-8820

http://www.laf.org

The LAF, a nonprofit organization founded by cancer survivor and cyclist Lance Armstrong, provides resources and support services to people diagnosed with cancer and their families. The LAF's services include Cycle of Hope, a national cancer education campaign for people with cancer and those at risk for developing the disease, and the Cancer Profiler, a free interactive treatment decision support tool. The LAF also provides scientific and research grants for the better understanding of cancer and cancer survivorship.

National Cancer Survivors Day Foundation (NCSD)
(615) 794-3006

ncsd@aol.com

http://www.ncsdf.org

National Cancer Survivors Day is the world's largest cancer survivor event and is celebrated on the first Sunday in June of each year in more than 700 communities throughout North America and elsewhere. A free celebration planning kit is available from the foundation.

National Coalition for Cancer Survivorship (NCCS)
1010 Wayne Avenue, Suite 770

Silver Spring, MD 20910-5600

(301) 650-9127

(877) 622-7937

info@canceradvocacy.org

http://www.canceradvocacy.org

NCCS is a network of groups and individuals that offer support to cancer survivors and their loved ones. It provides information and resources on cancer support advocacy and quality-of-life issues. A section of the NCCS Web site and a limited selection of publications are available in Spanish.

TESTICULAR CANCER
The Testicular Cancer Resource Center
A Web site devoted to raising public awareness and educating patients about diagnosis and treatment options. Features self-exam

instructions, dictionary, e-mail support, and questions to ask your doctor.

THYROID CANCER
American Thyroid Association
6066 Leesburg Pike, Suite 650
Falls Church, VA 22041
(703) 998-8890
http://www.thyroid.org

ThyCa: Thyroid Cancer Survivors Association, Inc.
P.O. Box 1545
New York, NY 10159-1545
(877) 588-7904
thyca@thyca.orgwww.thyca.org
A nonprofit organization providing information about thyroid cancer and support for thyroid cancer survivors. The Web site is maintained by thyroid cancer survivors.

The Thyroid Foundation of America
350 Ruth Sleeper Hall—RSL 350
40 Parkman Street
Boston, MA 02114
(800) 832-8321
(617) 726-8500
http://www.tsh.org

URINARY TRACT CANCERS
American Foundation for Urologic Disease (AFUD)
1000 Corporate Boulevard, Suite 410
Linthicum, MD 21090
(410) 689-3990
(800) 828-7866
http://www.afud.org
The AFUD supports research; provides education to patients, the general public, and health professionals; and offers patient support services for those who have or may be at risk for a urologic disease or disorder. They provide information on urologic disease and dysfunctions, including prostate cancer treatment options, bladder health, and sexual function. They also offer prostate cancer

*support groups (Prostate Cancer Network). Some Spanish-language
publications are available.*

VULVAR CANCER
The Vulvar Pain Foundation (VPF)
P.O. Drawer 177
Graham, NC 27253
(336) 226-0704
http://www.vulvarpainfoundation.org
*The Vulvar Pain Foundation is a nonprofit organization established
to end the isolation of women suffering from vulvar pain and
to give them hope, support, and reliable information in their
quest for freedom from pain. The network support is manned by
volunteers. There is a patient-to-patient network established by the
VPF either through telephone, correspondence, or support groups.
The network membership is at a yearly cost of $40.*

WISH FULFILLMENT GROUPS
The Dream Foundation
621 Chapala Street, Suite D
Santa Barbara, CA 93101-7011
(805) 564-2131
http://www.dreamfoundation.org
*The Dream Foundation tries to fulfill last wishes of terminal adults
(18–65) when life expectancy is less than one year.*

Make-A-Wish Foundation
2600 North Central Avenue, Suite 936
Phoenix, AZ 85013
(800) 722-9474
(602) 279-9474
http://www.wish.org
*MAWF is a foundation that grants "special wishes" to children
(ages 2½–18) who have a life-threatening illness. Services:
Devoted to fulfilling dreams; wish requests are granted; volunteer
services.*

The STARBRIGHT Foundation
11835 West Olympic Boulevard, Suite 500
Los Angeles, CA 90064
(310) 479-1212

http://www.starbright.org

The STARBRIGHT Foundation creates projects that are designed to help seriously ill children and adolescents cope with the psychosocial and medical challenges they face. The STARBRIGHT Foundation produces materials such as interactive educational CD-ROMs and videos about medical conditions and procedures, advice on talking with a health professional, and other issues related to children and adolescents who have serious medical conditions. All materials are available to children, adolescents, and their families free of charge. Staff can respond to calls in Spanish.

Starlight Children's Foundation
5900 Wilshire Boulevard, Suite 2530
Los Angeles, CA 90036
(323) 634-0080
(800) 274-7827
http://www.starlight.org

SCF grants the "special wishes" of critically, chronically, and/or terminally ill children ages four to 18. Services: Provides in-hospital entertainment, grants wishes to ill children, and plans family outings.

Sunshine Foundation
1041 Mill Creek Drive
Feaster Ville, PA 19053
(215) 396-4770
(800) 767-1976
http://www.sunshinefoundation.org

SFO grants the "special wishes" of critically, chronically, and/or terminally ill children, ages three to 21, whose families are under financial strain due to the child's illness. It is the original dream-granting organization.

APPENDIX 2

Headwear and Wig Mail-Order Options

HEADWEAR/CLOTHING

Hat and Soul
629 North Bush Street
Anaheim, CA 92805
(714) 991-4287
http://brownharrison.com/hatandsoul.shtml
Hat and Soul is a mail-order company specializing in hats for girls and women in chemotherapy.

Look Good . . . Feel Better for Teens
CTFA Foundation
1101 17th Street NW
Washington, DC 20036
(800) 395-5665
(202) 331-1770
http://www.lookgoodfeelbetter.org/audience/teens/program.htm
Look Good . . . Feel Better for Teens is a hospital-based public service program created by the CTFA and its partners to help girls and guys aged 13 to 17 deal with the appearance, health, and social side effects of cancer treatment. Launched in 1996, the program now offers on-site sessions in 16 cities, as well as the 2bMe Web site (http://www.2bme.org/2bMe.html) to reach teens everywhere. 2bMe is the online component of Look Good . . . Feel Better for Teens. The information-packed Web site covers all the nonmedical stuff teens with cancer wonder about—from skin and hair to fitness and friends. There are interactive style finder quizzes, how-to demos, and fashion slide shows. 2bMe is also recommended by Starbright World, the powerful hospital-to-hospital intranet for children with serious illnesses.

Soft Options
6345 Galletta Drive
Newark, CA 94560

(510) 300-5885

http://www.wearsoftoptions.com

This is a mail-order service for headwear. Soft Options developed a unisex cap that is fun and functional for kids of all ages! Whether the use is for recreation, fashion, or medical, a regular size cap fits most kids, and comes in a lot of fun patterns.

RESOURCES

American Brain Tumor Association

Hair and Wig Resource Web page

http://www.abta.org/siteFiles/SitePages/C6384C1547748A76FA99EE
   ABF8D12644.pdf

This Web site lists a variety of resources for wigs and headwear around the country.

WIGS

Locks of Love

2925 10th Avenue North, Suite 102

Lake Worth, FL 33461

(561) 963-1677

(888) 896-1588

http://www.locksoflove.org/

To request a hairpiece: http://www.locksoflove.org/request_
   hairpiece.php

Locks of Love is a nonprofit organization that provides hairpieces to financially disadvantaged children under age 18 suffering from medical hair loss. The organization uses donated hair to create the highest quality hair prosthetics.

APPENDIX 3

Cancer Centers

The National Cancer Institute (NCI) recognizes two types of centers: **Comprehensive Cancer Centers** and **Clinical Cancer Centers.** Each type of center has special characteristics and capabilities for organizing new programs of research that can take advantage of important new findings and research.

NCI-designated comprehensive cancer centers offer the most recent advances in cancer diagnosis and treatment, including participation in cancer clinical trials. These centers also provide community outreach and education programs about cancer. The benefits are up-to-date treatment, experienced health-care professionals, access to clinical trials, and probably a unit or associated center that performs stem cell transplantation, if needed.

Clinical cancer centers also offer the most up-to-date advances in cancer diagnosis and treatment, including participation in cancer clinical trials, but may not provide the same emphasis on educating the community about cancer prevention and control. The benefits are up-to-date treatment, experienced health-care professionals, access to clinical trials, and usually a unit or associated center that performs stem cell transplantation, if needed.

However, the terms Comprehensive Cancer Center and Clinical Cancer Center do not denote a difference in the *quality of care* they provide to patients.

* Comprehensive Cancer Centers
** Clinical Cancer Centers

ALABAMA
University of Alabama at Birmingham Comprehensive Cancer Center*
1824 Sixth Avenue South
Birmingham, AL 35294-3300

(205) 975-8222
(800) 822-0933
http://www.ccc.uab.edu

ARIZONA
Arizona Cancer Center*
The University of Arizona
1515 North Campbell Avenue
P.O. Box 245024
Tucson, AZ 85724
(520) 626-2900 (New Patient Registration Line)
(800) 622- COPE [2673]
http://www.azcc.arizona.edu

Mayo Clinic Cancer Center at Scottsdale*
13400 East Shea Boulevard
Scottsdale, AZ 85259
(480) 301-8484
(480) 301-1735 (appointment office)
http://www.mayoclinic.org/cancercenter

CALIFORNIA
The Burnham Institute**
10901 North Torrey Pines Road
La Jolla, CA 92037
(858) 646-3100
http://www.burnhaminstitute.org

Chao Family Comprehensive Cancer Center*
University of California at Irvine
Building 23, Route 81
101 The City Drive
Orange, CA 92868
(714) 456-8200
http://www.ucihs.uci.edu/cancer

City of Hope*
Cancer Center and Beckman Research Institute
1500 East Duarte Road
Duarte, CA 91010-3000
(626) 359-8111

(800) 826-HOPE [4673]
becomingapatient@coh.org
http://www.cityofhope.org

Jonsson Comprehensive Cancer Center at UCLA*
8–684 Factor Building
UCLA Box 951781
Los Angeles, CA 90095-1781
(310) 825-5268
jcccinfo@mednet.ucla.edu
http://www.cancer.mednet.ucla.edu

The Salk Institute for Biological Studies**
P.O. Box 85800
10010 North Torrey Pines Road
La Jolla, CA 92037
(858) 453-4100
http://www.salk.edu

UC Davis Cancer Center**
University of California, Davis
4501 X Street
Sacramento, CA 95817
(800) 362-5566 (patient referral)
(916) 734-5900
http://cancer.ucdmc.ucdavis.edu

UC San Diego Cancer Center*
9500 Gilman Drive
La Jolla, CA 92093-0658
(858) 534-7600
http://cancer.ucsd.edu

UC San Francisco Comprehensive Cancer Center*
Box 0128, UCSF
2340 Sutter Street
San Francisco, CA 94143-0128
(415) 476-2201 (general information)
(800) 888-8664 (cancer referral line)
referral.center@ucsfmedicalcenter.org
http://cc.ucsf.edu

USC/Norris Comprehensive Cancer Center and Hospital*
1441 Eastlake Avenue
Los Angeles, CA 90033-0804
(323) 865-3000
(800) USC-CARE [872-2273]
cainfo@ccnt.hsc.usc.edu
http://ccnt.hsc.usc.edu

COLORADO
University of Colorado Cancer Center*
Box F–704
1665 North Ursula Street
Aurora, CO 80010
(720) 848-0300
(800) 473-2288 (cancer referral line)
http://www.uccc.info

CONNECTICUT
Yale Cancer Center*
Yale University School of Medicine
333 Cedar Street
P.O. Box 208028
New Haven, CT 06520-8028
(203) 785-4095 (administrative offices)
http://www.info.med.yale.edu/ycc

DISTRICT OF COLUMBIA
Lombardi Cancer Center*
Georgetown University Medical Center
3800 Reservoir Road NW
Washington, DC 20007
(202) 784-4000
http://lombardi.georgetown.edu

FLORIDA
**H. Lee Moffitt Cancer Center & Research Institute at
   The University of South Florida***
12902 Magnolia Drive
Tampa, FL 33612-9497
(813) 972-HOPE [4673]
http://www.moffitt.usf.edu

Mayo Clinic Cancer Center—Jacksonville*
4500 San Pablo Road
Jacksonville, FL 32224
(904) 953-2272
(904) 953-2300 (TTD)
http://www.mayoclinic.org/cancercenter

HAWAII
Cancer Research Center of Hawaii**
1236 Lauhala Street
Honolulu, HI 96813
(808) 586-3010
http://www.crch.org

ILLINOIS
The Robert H. Lurie Comprehensive Cancer Center*
Northwestern University
Olson Pavilion 8250
710 North Fairbanks Court
Chicago, IL 60611-3013
(312) 908-5250
cancer@northwestern.edu
http://cancer.northwestern.edu/home/index.cfm

University of Chicago Cancer Research Center*
Mail Code 2115
5841 South Maryland Avenue
Chicago, IL 60637-1470
(773) 702-9200
(888) 824-0200 (new patients)
http://www-uccrc.uchicago.edu

INDIANA
Indiana University Cancer Center**
535 Barnhill Drive
Indianapolis, IN 46202-5289
(317) 278-4822
(888) 600-4822
http://iucc.iu.edu

Purdue Cancer Center**
Hansen Life Sciences Research Building
Purdue University
201 South University Street
West Lafayette, IN 47907-2064
(765) 494-9129
http://www.cancer.purdue.edu

IOWA
**The Holden Comprehensive Cancer Center at The University
of Iowa***
Room 5970–Z JPP
200 Hawkins Drive
Iowa City, IA 52242-1009
(800) 777-8442 (patient referral)
(800) 237-1225 (general information)
Cancer-Center@uiowa.edu
http://www.uihealthcare.com

MAINE
The Jackson Laboratory**
600 Main Street
Bar Harbor, ME 04609-0800
(207) 288-6000 (main)
(207) 288-6051 (public information)
pubinfo@jax.org
http://www.jax.org

MARYLAND
**Sidney Kimmel Comprehensive Cancer Center at
Johns Hopkins***
The Harry and Jeanette Weinberg Building
Suite 1100
401 North Broadway
Baltimore, MD 21231-2410
(410) 955-8964 (patient referral)
(410) 955-8804 (clinical trials)
http://www.hopkinskimmelcancercenter.org

MASSACHUSETTS
Dana-Farber Cancer Institute*
44 Binney Street
Boston, MA 02115
(617) 632-3000 (ask for patient information)
http://www.dana-farber.org

MIT Center for Cancer Research**
Room E17–110
Massachusetts Institute of Technology
77 Massachusetts Avenue
Cambridge, MA 02139-4307
(617) 253-8511
http://web.mit.edu/ccr

MICHIGAN
Barbara Ann Karmanos Cancer Institute*
Operating the Meyer L. Prentis Comprehensive Cancer Center of
  Metropolitan Detroit
Wertz Clinical Center
4100 John R Street
Detroit, MI 48201-1379
(800) KARMANOS [527-6266]
info@karmanos.org
http://www.karmanos.org

University of Michigan Comprehensive Cancer Center*
1500 East Medical Center Drive
Ann Arbor, MI 48109
(800) 865-1125
wwwcancer@umich.edu
http://www.cancer.med.umich.edu

MINNESOTA
Mayo Clinic Cancer Center*
200 First Street SW
Rochester, MN 55905
(507) 284-2111 (appointment information desk)
http://www.mayo.edu/cancercenter

University of Minnesota Cancer Center*
Mayo Mail Code 806
420 Delaware Street SE
Minneapolis, MN 55455
(612) 624-8484
info@cancer.umn.edu
http://www.cancer.umn.edu

MISSOURI

Siteman Cancer Center**
Barnes-Jewish Hospital and Washington University School of Medicine
Box 8100
660 South Euclid
St. Louis, MO 63110-1093
(314) 747-7222
(800) 600-3606
http://www.siteman.wustl.edu

NEBRASKA

UNMC Eppley Cancer Center**
University of Nebraska Medical Center
986805 Nebraska Medical Center
Omaha, NE 68198-6805
(402) 559-4238
http://www.unmc.edu/cancercenter

NEW HAMPSHIRE

Norris Cotton Cancer Center*
Dartmouth-Hitchcock Medical Center
One Medical Center Drive
Lebanon, NH 03756-0002
(603) 650-6300 (administration)
(800) 639-6918 (cancer help line)
cancerhelp@dartmouth.edu
http://www.cancer.dartmouth.edu/index.shtml

NEW JERSEY

The Cancer Institute of New Jersey**
Robert Wood Johnson Medical School
195 Little Albany Street

New Brunswick, NJ 08901
(732) 235-CINJ [2465]
http://www.cinj.org

NEW MEXICO
UNM Cancer Research and Treatment Center**
University of New Mexico Health Sciences Center
MSC 08 4630
900 Camino de Salud NE
Albuquerque, NM 87131-0001
(505) 272-4946
(800) 432-6806
http://cancer.unm.edu

NEW YORK
Albert Einstein Cancer Center*
Albert Einstein College of Medicine
1300 Morris Park Avenue
Bronx, NY 10461
(718) 430-2302
aeccc@aecom.yu.edu
http://www.aecom.yu.edu/cancer

Cold Spring Harbor Laboratory**
P.O. Box 100
One Bungtown Road
Cold Spring Harbor, NY 11724
(516) 367-8397
http://www.cshl.org

Herbert Irving Comprehensive Cancer Center*
Columbia Presbyterian Center
New York–Presbyterian Hospital
PH 18, Room 200
622 West 168th Street
New York, NY 10032
(212) 305-9327 (office of administration)
http://www.ccc.columbia.edu

Memorial Sloan-Kettering Cancer Center*
1275 York Avenue
New York, NY 10021

(800) 525-2225
http://www.mskcc.org

NYU Cancer Institute**
New York University Cancer Institute
550 First Avenue
New York, NY 10016
(212) 263-6485
http://www.nyucancerinstitute.org

Roswell Park Cancer Institute*
Elm and Carlton Streets
Buffalo, NY 14263-0001
(800) ROSWELL [767-9355]
http://www.roswellpark.org

NORTH CAROLINA
Comprehensive Cancer Center of Wake Forest University*
Wake Forest University Baptist Medical Center
Medical Center Boulevard
Winston-Salem, NC 27157-1082
(336) 716-4464
http://www.bgsm.edu/cancer

Duke Comprehensive Cancer Center*
Duke University Medical Center
Box 3843
301 MSRB
Durham, NC 27710
(919) 684-3377
http://www.cancer.duke.edu

UNC Lineberger Comprehensive Cancer Center*
School of Medicine
University of North Carolina at Chapel Hill
Campus Box 7295
Chapel Hill, NC 27599-7295
(919) 966-3036
dgs@med.unc.edu
http://cancer.med.unc.edu

OHIO
Ireland Cancer Center*
University Hospitals of Cleveland
11100 Euclid Avenue
Cleveland, OH 44106-5065
(216) 844-5432
(800) 641-2422
http://www.irelandcancercenter.org

The Ohio State University Comprehensive Cancer Center*
The Arthur G. James Cancer Hospital and
  Richard J. Solove Research Institute, Suite 519
300 West 10th Avenue
Columbus, OH 43210-1240
(800) 293-5066 (The James Line)
cancerinfo@jamesline.com
http://www.jamesline.com

OREGON
The OHSU Cancer Institute**
The Oregon Health Sciences University Cancer Institute
CR145
3181 Southwest Sam Jackson Park Road
Portland, OR 97201-3098
(503) 494-1617
cancer@ohsu.edu
http://www.ohsucancer.com

PENNSYLVANIA
Abramson Cancer Center of the University of Pennsylvania*
15th Floor, Penn Tower
3400 Spruce Street
Philadelphia, PA 19104-4283
(215) 662-4000 (main)
(800) 789-PENN [7366] (referral/schedule an appointment)
http://www.penncancer.org

Fox Chase Cancer Center*
333 Cottman Avenue
Philadelphia, PA 19111

(215) 728-2570 (to schedule an appointment)
(888) FOX CHASE [369-2427]
http://www.fccc.edu

Kimmel Cancer Center**
Thomas Jefferson University
Bluemle Life Sciences Building
233 South 10th Street
Philadelphia, PA 19107-5541
(215) 503-4500
(800) 533-3669 (Jefferson Cancer Network)
(800) 654-5984 (TDD)
http://www.kimmelcancercenter.org

University of Pittsburgh Cancer Institute*
5150 Centre Avenue
Pittsburgh, PA 15232
(412) 647-2811
PCI-INFO@upmc.edu
http://www.upci.upmc.edu

Wistar Institute**
3601 Spruce Street
Philadelphia, PA 19104
(215) 898-3700
http://www.wistar.org

TENNESSEE
St. Jude Children's Research Hospital**
332 North Lauderdale Street
Memphis, TN 38105-2794
(901) 495-3300
http://www.stjude.org

The Vanderbilt-Ingram Cancer Center*
Vanderbilt University
649 The Preston Building
Nashville, TN 37232-6838
(615) 936-1782; 615-936-5847; or 800-811-8480 (Clinical trial or
    treatment option information)
(888) 488-4089 (all other calls)
http://www.vicc.org

TEXAS
San Antonio Cancer Institute*
7703 Floyd Curl Drive
San Antonio, TX 78229
(210) 567-2710
http://saci.uthscsa.edu

The University of Texas M.D. Anderson Cancer Center*
1515 Holcombe Boulevard
Houston, TX 77030
(713) 792-6161
(800) 392-1611
http://www.mdanderson.org

UTAH
Huntsman Cancer Institute**
University of Utah
2000 Circle of Hope
Salt Lake City, UT 84112
(801) 585-0303
(877) 585-0303
http://www.hci.utah.edu

VERMONT
Vermont Cancer Center*
University of Vermont
Medical Alumni Building
Burlington, VT 05401
(802) 656-4414
vcc@uvm.edu
http://www.vermontcancer.org

VIRGINIA
The Cancer Center at The University of Virginia**
University of Virginia Health System
Box 800334
Charlottesville, VA 22908
(804) 924-9333
(800) 223-9173
http://www.healthsystem.virginia.edu/internet/cancer

Massey Cancer Center**
Virginia Commonwealth University
401 College Street
P.O. Box 980037
Richmond, VA 23298-0037
(804) 828-0450
http://www.vcu.edu/mcc

WASHINGTON
Fred Hutchinson Cancer Research Center*
LA–205
P.O. Box 19024
1100 Fairview Avenue North
Seattle, WA 98109-1024
(206) 288-1024
(800) 804-8824 (appointments and medical referral—Seattle Cancer
    Care Alliance)
hutchdoc@seattlecca.org (patient information)
http://www.fhcrc.org

WISCONSIN
University of Wisconsin Comprehensive Cancer Center*
600 Highland Avenue, K5/601
Madison, WI 53792-6164
(608) 263-8600
(608) 262-5223; (800) 622-8922 (Cancer Connect)
uwccc@uwcc.wisc.edu
http://www.cancer.wisc.edu

APPENDIX 4
Camps for Kids with Cancer

GENERAL INFORMATION
American Cancer Society—Silver Spring Office
11331 Amherst Avenue
Silver Spring, MD 20902
(301) 933-9350
http://www.cancer.org
Provides information, education, advocacy, and patient services,
including transportation, children's camps, assistance and support
groups such as Look Good . . . Feel Better.

Brave Kids: Camps and Resources for Children with Chronic,
Life-Threatening Illnesses or Disabilities
http://www.bravekids.org
Provides information about camping resources for kids with cancer.

Camp List for Children with Cancer
The Candlelighters Childhood Cancer Foundation
National Office
P.O. Box 498
Kensington, MD 20895-0498
(800) 366-2223
(301) 962-3520
info@candlelighters.org
http://www.candlelighters.org/supportcamps.stm

Camp Quality USA
http://www.campqualityusa.org
A summer camping experience and year-round support program for
children with cancer.

Camps 2006: A Directory of Camps and Summer Programs for Children and Youth with Special Needs and Disabilities in the Metro New York Area
Resources for Children with Special Needs
Publications/Department B
116 East 16th Street, 5th Floor
New York, NY 10003
(212) 677-4650
info@resourcesnyc.org
http://www.resourcesnyc.org

Children's Oncology Camping Association International
http://www.coca-intl.org
A listing of approximately 65 camps in the United States and others elsewhere in the world that have camps for cancer kids.

National Camp Association, Inc.
610 Fifth Avenue
P.O. Box 5371
New York, NY 10185
(800) 966-CAMP [2267]
(212) 645-0653
info@summercamp.org
http://www.summercamp.org
CampQuest, an online camp selection guide, is available on the NCA Web site.

ALABAMA
Camp Rap-A-Hope
2701 Airport Boulevard
Mobile, AL 36606
(251) 476-9880
rapahope@earthlink.net
http://www.msomc.com/camp_rap.htm
Specialty camp for children with cancer, featuring beautiful setting and medical support. No charge to campers. Overnight camp, coed, from seven to 17, one-week sessions. Activities include archery, canoeing, field trips, golf, horseback riding, kayaking, leadership development, SCUBA, recreational swimming, team building, aquatic activities, arts and crafts, basketball, and music.

ARIZONA
Dream Street Foundation—Canyon Ranch Camp (in Tucson, AZ)
9536 Wilshire Boulevard, Suite 310
Beverly Hills, CA 90212
(562) 933-3350
dreamstreetca@aol.com
http://www.dreamstreetfoundation.org
*Canyon Ranch is a program designed to help meet the special needs
of maturing young people with life-threatening diseases. Funded
by the Dream Street Foundation, young people with cancer
and other serious illnesses are given the opportunity to briefly
escape their complex lives and medical problems to prepare for
the transition from adolescents to adulthood. At present, the
Dream Street Foundation sponsors two Canyon Ranch sessions in
Tucson, Arizona. The participants are flown in from around the
United States, Europe, Canada, and Mexico. The Canyon Ranch
program is free of charge to its many young participants and is
supported by volunteer counselors and medical staff.*

CALIFORNIA
Camp Rainbow
6535 Wilshire Boulevard 120
Los Angeles, CA 90048
(323) 655-7741
http://www.csmc.edu/3338.html
*One-week summer camp for kids with cancer that offers archery,
arts and crafts, baseball/softball, ceramics/pottery, drama, hiking,
horseback riding, nature/environment studies, and recreational
swimming. Camp season begins in August and ends in August.
Sessions are one week for coed children ages seven to 17.*

Camp Reach for the Stars
250 West Citrus Grove Lane, Suite 260
Oxnard, CA 93036
(805) 278-6100
Jennifer.Finnerty@cancer.org
http://www.cancer.org
*Camp Reach for the Stars offers children with cancer and their
families (no charge) the chance to attend a camp staffed by
health-care professionals in a lovely forest and ocean setting.*

Activities include campfire activities, tide pool exploration, arts and crafts, children and teen activities, entertainment, support groups, spa day.

Camp Ronald McDonald for Good Times
Coachella Valley Office: Camp Ronald McDonald for Good
901 East Tahquitz Canyon Way, C201
Palm Springs, CA 92262
(800) 625-7295
info@campronaldmcdonald.org
http://www.campronaldmcdonald.org/
Conducts summer and winter camps for young cancer patients as well as spring and fall family camps for families who have a child with cancer; sibling camps provide the same fun and support for the brothers and sisters of camper patients. Programs include all of the traditional elements of a camp; swimming, horseback riding, hiking, backpacking, and sports that can be adapted, as needed, to ensure that each person is able to participate, regardless of his or her level of challenge.

Camp Shiwaka
7070 East Carson Street
Long Beach, CA 90808
(562) 421-2725
campfirelb@earthlink.net
http://www.campfirelb.org
Camp Shiwaka runs for three weeks out of the summer for all children. Also provides Camp Sommersault Day camp with one-week sessions for cancer patients and their families. Activities for both camps include cooking, outdoor activities, arts and crafts, and games.

Okizu Foundation—Family Camp
16 Digital Drive
Novato, CA 94949
(415) 382-9083
info@okizu.org
http://www.okizu.org/family.html
Family Camp is an experience designed to give parents and children with disabilities/cancer a few days of fun, play, and relaxation. It is a chance to "get away" for a few days with other families who know what your experiences have been like. Medical staff from various hospitals will be on site during Family Camp. Meals are

*planned and prepared by a qualified cook and served family style,
so there is no need to worry about cooking. Healthy snacks are
served during the morning and afternoon each day.*

Okizu Foundation—Oncology Camp
16 Digital Drive
Novato, CA 94949
(415) 382-9083
info@okizu.org
http://www.okizu.org/oncology.html
*The resident camp program allows the campers to experience fun,
adventure, independence, camaraderie, and learning in an
outdoor setting. The planning of activities is done by the campers
in their cabin group under the guidance of a trained counselor.
Expert medical supervision is provided by the pediatric oncology
departments, social workers, and recreation therapists from the
participating hospitals. All prescription medications (oral, inhaled,
inject, and intravenous) are administered at camp as needed, on
schedule, by licensed nurses and physicians.*

Okizu Foundation—Siblings Camp
16 Digital Drive
Novato, CA 94949
(415) 382-9083
info@okizu.org
http://www.okizu.org/siblings.html
*Recognizing that childhood cancer affects the entire family, the Okizu
Foundation provides a camp for the siblings of a child with cancer.
SIBS (Special and Important Brothers and Sisters) Camp meets the
often neglected needs that healthy children can have during their
sibling's treatment.*

Okizu Foundation—Teens n' Twenties (TNT) Camp
16 Digital Drive
Novato, CA 94949
(415) 382-9083
info@okizu.org
http://www.okizu.org/tnt.html
*The Teens n' Twenties (TNT) program operates several times each
year, providing weekend recreation and support programs for the
older patients and siblings. These weekends provide the teenagers
and young adults with an ongoing opportunity to strengthen their
friendships and give and receive support from their peers.*

The Orange County Camp for Oncology Children
OCF-OCF
P.O. Box 6023
Orange, CA 92863
(949) 855-1972
ksullivan@ocf-ocf.org
http://www.ocf-ocf.org/main.htm
Through recreational and social activities, the Orange County Camp
    brings together families facing similar struggles, dealing with the
    illness of a child, in a relaxed, comfortable environment where
    they can share burdens and offer each other support and hope.
    OCF-OCF serves the families of pediatric cancer patients who reside
    in or receive their treatment in Orange County, California. The
    kids, their siblings, and their parents are treated to trips to local
    amusement parks and sporting events and a blowout holiday
    party in December.

COLORADO
First Descents
P.O. Box 2193
Vail, CO 81658
(970) 476-9400
info@firstdescents.org
http://www.firstdescents.com
First Descents is a cost-free kayak and adventure camp for young
    adults, ages 14 to 25, who have or have had cancer. Founded
    by professional kayaker Brad Ludden in 2000, First Descents
    uses kayaking and other outdoor activities to help campers face
    challenges and obstacles associated with living with cancer in a
    fun and supportive environment. Three weeks of camp are offered
    at the 7W Guest Ranch outside of Vail, Colorado. First Descents
    has applicants from all over the country and travel scholarships
    are provided upon need.

CONNECTICUT
Hole in the Wall Gang Camp
565 Ashford Center Road
Ashford, CT 06278
(860) 429-3444
ashford@holeinthewallgang.org
http://www.holeinthewallgang.org

The Hole in the Wall Gang Camp, founded by Paul Newman, is a nonprofit residential summer camp, a dazzlingly equipped Wild West hideout in northeastern Connecticut, where children with cancer or other serious blood diseases do not have to sit on the sidelines. More than 1,000 children from seven to 15 years old come each year, free of charge, from across the United States and abroad. Offering nine summer sessions, the Hole in the Wall Gang Camp also provides year-round activities for campers and other seriously ill children and their siblings at camp and in their own communities. Camp-sponsored programs provide health-care professionals and social workers with support and training. Retreats are organized for the children's parents at resorts around the country offering respite, counseling, mutual support, and positive activities, free of charge.

FLORIDA
Boggy Creek Camp
30500 Brantley Branch Road
Eustis, FL 32736
(352) 483-4200
info@boggycreek.org
http://www.boggycreek.org
Permanent year-round facility where young people between ages seven and 16 with chronic and life-threatening illnesses can come at no charge to them or their families. Transportation to and from the camp is usually the family's responsibility. However, many local health organizations, such as the American Heart and American Lung associations and American Cancer Society, will help with the cost and coordination of travel plans. All campers attend free of charge and are encouraged to ride the American Cancer Society's free chartered buses. Activities include camping, swimming, music, arts and crafts, archery, sports, fishing, talent shows, horseback riding, and campfires.

Camp Florida Fish Tales, Inc
P.O. Box 21682
Sarasota, FL 34276
(941) 921-9182
info@campflafishtales.com
http://www.campflafishtales.com
Camp Florida Fish Tales is a weeklong, barrier-free, wheelchair-accessible camp which is available to all children with medical or physical disabilities. At Florida Fish Tales campers learn to deal

with their own emotional and physical limitations while enjoying such activities as swimming, fishing, archery, pet therapy, arts and crafts, games, and group activities. Every child has his or her own "special" camp counselor.

Camp Good Days & Special Times, Inc.—Tampa
1311 North Westshore Boulevard, Suite 314
Tampa, FL 33607
(813) 281-2192
tampa@campgooddays.org
http://www.campgooddays.org
A residential camping program that provides children with cancer ages seven to 17 the opportunity to develop growth and self-confidence through shared experiences in a supportive and loving environment.

Children's Miracle Network—Miracle Camp
9840 Beulah Road 32526
Pensacola, FL 32526
(850) 944-1677
bulander@shhpens.org
http://www.sacred-heart.org/miraclecamp1.asp
For children with chronic or life-threatening illnesses, respite, peace, and renewal, provided through Sacred Heart Children's Hospital. The camp is located northwest of Pensacola. Miracle Camp provides therapeutic camp experiences and educational and supportive programs. The American Lung Association provides transportation to and from camp.

Foundation for Dreams, Inc.—Dream Oaks Camp
2620 Manatee Avenue W, Suite D
Bradenton, FL 34205
(941) 748-8809
info@foundationfordreams.org
http://www.foundationfordreams.org/program.asp
Dream Oaks Camp provides programs for children with chronic serious illnesses by offering camping experiences on weekends, at day camp and at resident camp. Children accepted range in ages seven to 17 of all levels of disability, illness, and developmental conditions.

Good Hope Equestrian Training Center Children's Oncology Camp
22155 SW 147th Avenue
Miami, FL 33170

(305) 258-2838
ghetc@bellsouth.net
http://www.goodhopeequestriancenter.com
*This place is where children (as well as their siblings) can come and,
for a few weeks out of the year, forget about their ailments and
remember how to be kids through therapeutic interventions such
as summer camps.*

**Miami Children's Hospital—United Order True Sisters Special
  Clinic Camp**
Miami, FL 33155
(305) 662-8360
http://www.mch.com/
*A seven-day sleepaway camp for children ages seven to 17 who have
been stricken with cancer. The camp helps the children develop
a sense of self-reliance and strength—in addition to being a lot
of fun. The camp has continuous on-site nursing and medical
coverage and is run by the division of hematology-oncology.*

GEORGIA
Camp Twin Lakes
600 Means Street
Suite 110
Atlanta, GA 30318
(404) 231-9887
info@camptwinlakes.org
camptwinlakes@mindspring.com
http://www.camptwinlakes.org
*An accredited member of the American Camping Association, Camp
Twin Lakes summer camping facility serves 14 summer camps for
children with special medical needs, including cancer.*

MAINE
Camp Sunshine
35 Acadia Road
Casco, ME 04015
(207) 655-3800
info@campsunshine.org
http://www.campsunshine.com
*A camp that offers weeklong camping for the entire family who has
a child with cancer. There are workshops, recreational activities,*

and medical support available. Camp Sunshine supports children with life-threatening illnesses and their families. The camp addresses the impact of a life-threatening illness on every member of the immediate family—the ill child, the parents, and the siblings. Free quality services are provided at the camp, including accommodations and meals, on-site medical services, counseling services, and recreational facilities. Each family is sponsored by an individual, civic group, corporation, or foundation, which enables a family to spend a week at Camp Sunshine free of charge.

MARYLAND
Camp Sunrise
Camp Hidden Valley
4722 Mellow Road
White Hall, MD 21161
(410) 931-6850 (American Cancer Society Maryland Div.)
http://www.cancer.org

Camp for children with cancer, ages four to 18 years old. One week each August. Offers two programs for cancer patients: day camp for four–five year olds and a residential camp for six–18 year olds. Residential camp offers swimming, tennis, clowning, dancing, etc. Team of oncologists/nurses on hand 24 hours a day. Also offers separate weekend camps for siblings and young adults who are current and former cancer patients, ages 18 to 25. Transportation provided.

Carol Jean Cancer Foundation, Inc.—Camp Friendship
4019 Damascus Road
Gaithersburg, MD 20882
(301) 774-0130 (summer only)
cjcfkids@aol.com
http://www.cjcf4kids.org/default.asp

Special weeklong residential camp for children with cancer that is designed especially with their needs in mind. Activities include softball, archery, badminton, volleyball, tennis, basketball, shuffleboard, hopscotch, swimming, canoeing, kayaking, paddleboats, nature train, and mini putt-putt course. All campers are being treated at area hospitals.

Sun Sibs Camp
Camp Hidden Valley
4722 Mellow Road

White Hall, MD 21161
(410) 931-6850
http://www.cancer.org
Recognizes siblings of children with cancer have special needs too. Sibling Camping weekend, one weekend per year. Includes traditional camping activities.

MISSISSIPPI
Camp Hopewell—Christians Living with Cancer Camp
24 County Road 231
Oxford, MS 38655
(662) 234-2254
info@camphopewell.com
http://www.camphopewell.com/christiansliving.html
Offered by Camp Hopewell, this is a free summer camp for children with cancer and their immediate families. Scheduled activities allow parents and siblings to relax and have fun together in a low-stress environment. Professional medical staff are onsite to help with any medical needs.

Camp Rainbow—MS
1380 Livingston Lane
Jackson, MS 39213
(601) 362-8874
betsy.belk@cancer.org
http://www.cancer.org
Sponsored by the American Cancer Society, this camping experience is for children (ages six to 17) with cancer, from any county in Mississippi. Camp Rainbow is located at Henry S. Jacobs Camp in Utica, Mississippi.

MONTANA
Camp Make a Dream
http://www.campdream.org
A camp with programs for cancer kids, siblings, teens, and young adult camp experiences.

NEW JERSEY
Camp Quality New Jersey
P.O. Box 264
Adelphia, NJ 07710

(732) 780-1409
frankd@campqualitynj.org
http://www.campqualitynj.org
*Camp Quality New Jersey is a nonprofit, tax-exempt, charitable
organization providing a free weeklong camping experience and
support program for children with cancer. Camp Quality frees
children with cancer from their hospital/physician environment
and allows them to enjoy themselves in an outdoor environment
where they can forget about their illness. On-site medical
staff and adult volunteers supervise the activities and provide
companionship for the children. Additional support programs
continuing throughout the year include reunions, family outings,
and family financial assistance.*

Happiness Is Camping
62 Sunset Lake Road
Blairstown, NJ 07825
(908) 362-6733
hicamping@nac.net
http://www.happinessiscamping.org
*Happiness Is Camping, for children with cancer. About 400
children, girls and boys ages six to 16 years, attend the overnight
camp, staying from one to six weeks. There are six summer
sessions. The camp is free to all, supported by donations and
volunteer staff members. The medical staff, doctors and nurses,
all from Memorial Sloan-Kettering Cancer Center, provide
medical supervision of the highest quality, with facilities for kids
requiring chemotherapy, at risk of bleeding and infection, or with
significant physical disabilities.*

NEW YORK
Camp Adventure
American Cancer Society
Northport, NY 11768
(212) 586-8700
mesolen@wsboces.org
http://www.cancer.org
*Sponsored by the American Cancer Society, Camp Adventure provides
an opportunity for kids to just be kids while receiving the medical
attention they need from pediatric oncology professionals. The
camp also provides children with support from other kids who*

*have undergone or are undergoing treatment. Daily activities are
designed to meet the special needs of campers, while challenging
them and fostering independence and self-confidence. Programs
include sports, arts and crafts, swimming, nature activities,
snorkeling, boating, archery, karate, kite-making, and the camp
newsletter, and each night is filled with theme dances, talent
shows, parties, and more.*

Camp Good Days & Special Times
1332 Pittsford-Mendon Road
Mendon, NY 14506
(716) 206-0709
http://www.campgooddays.org
btobin@campgooddays.org
*Day and residential programs for children and their siblings who are
dealing with cancer.*

Camp Simcha
151 30th Street
New York, NY 10001
(212) 465-1300
http://www.chailifeline.org
http://www.chailifeline.org/camp_simcha.asp
*A kosher camp for Jewish children with cancer in New York. Situated
on 125 acres in Glen Spey, New York, Camp Simcha offers kosher
summer camping for children with cancer and other catastrophic
illnesses. Activities offered include miniature golf, swimming,
crafts, rocketry, photography, drama, pottery, woodworking,
computers, music, dance, and karate. Every summer the camp
holds four or five concerts starring popular entertainers. On-site
24-hour medical supervision. Campers must be at least six years of
age. Stay, including transportation from anywhere in the world, is
completely free of charge. A nominal registration fee is required.*

NORTH CAROLINA
Camp Carefree
275 Carefree Lane
Stokesdale, NC 27357
(336) 427-0966
tscottmichelle@hughes.net
http://www.CampCarefree.org

A free summer camp for children with chronic illnesses and disabilities. An opportunity for children to participate in a normal camp environment with adapted activities. Camp Carefree is a place where kids just get to be kids.

TENNESSEE
Angel Heart Farm
9840 Sam Donald Road
Nolensville, TN 37135
(615) 566-4976
http://www.angelheartfarm.org
Angel Heart Farm, Inc., is a therapeutic program that uses equine-assisted therapy for children with chronic and life-threatening illnesses and their families. This therapy can improve one's mental and physical health, shorten recovery time, and decrease stress and incidents of depression in children. Through interaction with animals, children are empowered to be caregivers instead of care recipients.

East Tennessee Children's Hospital—Camp Eagles' Nest
c/o ETCH Hematology Clinic
842 Gleason Road
Knoxville, TN 37919
(865) 541-8476
care@etch.com
http://www.etch.com/tourcamps.cfm
For patients from the East Tennessee Children's Hematology/Oncology Clinic, Camp Eagles' Nest offers campers a full week in June to enjoy the outdoors by riding horses, canoeing, rock climbing, tubing down the river, and more. This program is free of charge. Camp takes place at the Wesley Woods Camp in Townsend.

TEXAS
Camp C.A.M.P. (Children's Association for Maximum Potential)
P.O. Box 27086
San Antonio, TX 78227
(210) 292-3566
campmail@sprynet.com
http://www.campcamp.org
CAMP offers a chance for children to enjoy nature, new activities, residential camping, and new friends and a chance for the parents

to relax, enjoy each other, and take a break from around-the-clock caregiving responsibilities one experiences when raising a child with complex medical conditions.

VIRGINIA
Camp Holiday Trails
400 Holiday Trails Lane
Charlottesville, VA 22903
(434) 977-3781
holidaytrails@nexet.net
http://avenue.org/cht
Summer camp for children with special health needs. Campers range in age from seven to 14, and there is a Blazer program for kids ages 15 to 17. Medical diagnoses vary. Activites include archery, horseback riding, swimming, canoeing, wilderness education, arts and crafts, athletics, and organized games.

Special Love, Inc.
117 Youth Development Court
Winchester, VA 22602
(540) 667-3774
lcain@visuallink.com
http://www.speciallove.org
Offers various camp programs for children with cancer.

Special Love, Inc.—Camp Fantastic
117 Youth Development Court
Winchester, VA 22602
(540) 667-3774
dsmith@visuallink.com
http://www.speciallove.org
Offers a week of summer fun to children with cancer, ages seven to 17, who are currently being treated or have undergone treatment within three years. Provides classes, recreation, theme parties, campfires, and other exciting activities. Full medical staff on site.

WASHINGTON
Camp Goodtimes—American Cancer Society
2120 First Avenue North
Seattle, WA 98109
(206) 283-1152

http://www.cancer.org

Camp Goodtimes is a weeklong camp for children with cancer and their siblings. Around-the-clock health care is provided for each child. The camp is for children ages seven to 17. Usually takes place the final week of June or first week of July. Activities include canoeing, swimming, hiking, bicycling, outdoor games, arts and crafts, and fishing.

Camp Prime Time
P.O. Box 148
Yakima, WA 98907
(509) 248-2854
primetime@nwinfo.net
http://www.campprimetime.org

Provides a wilderness facility for families of children with serious/ terminal illnesses or disabilities. The whole family comes to camp and there is no charge. The camping experience runs from Friday to Sunday and serves groups from all parts of the Pacific Northwest. They have 14 cabins, provide all meals, offer a boat ride on Clear Lake (wheelchair accessible), have a campfire with s'mores, horseback riding, lots of trails to explore, and fishing poles to be used. They serve a broad range of disabilities and illnesses. No medical facility on site. Closest hospital is one hour away. Serves groups from all parts of the Pacific Northwest.

Kids N Cancer—Camp Agape Northwest
2100 Boyer Avenue East
Seattle, WA 98112
(206) 783-4466

Provides various camp activities and outdoor experiences to kids ages four to 16 years old with cancer and their families.

WEST VIRGINIA
Camp WINACA
YMCA Camp Horseshoe
Rte 2 Box 138
Parsons, WV 26287
(304) 296-8155
mary.lough@cancer.org
http://www.cancer.org

Camp for children with cancer seven to 16 years old. Provides a safe environment to learn standard camping skills. Provides the opportunity to develop a self-sufficient attitude, self-esteem, and a sense of responsibility. One-week camp that offers swimming, sports, hikes, fishing, arts and crafts, riflery, and campfire fun. Team of oncologists and nurses are on hand 24/7. Transportation to and from camp is provided.

GLOSSARY

adjuvant chemotherapy   Chemotherapy that destroys very small cells left behind after a tumor has been removed. This may prevent a recurrence.

antiemetic   A medicine that controls or prevents nausea and vomiting.

B cells   White blood cells (also called B lymphocytes) that make antibodies that are formed in bone marrow. They are an important part of the body's immune system.

biopsy   A test in which a tissue sample is removed from a suspicious mass to check for cancer, either with a long needle (needle biopsy) or via a small cut (surgical biopsy).

blood-brain barrier   A closely spaced network of blood vessels that makes it physically difficult for certain potentially toxic substances to enter the brain. This can be a good thing (keeping poisons out of the brain), but it can be less helpful if it prevents medicines from entering the brain.

B lymphocytes   *See* B cells.

bone marrow aspiration   A test of a small sample of cells removed from a bone (usually the hip bone).

carcinoma   The most common of five types of basic cancer that first appears in the tissues lining the surface or cavity of the skin, including mucous membranes, lungs, bladder, nerves, and so on. They include carcinoma, leukemia, lymphoma, myeloma, and sarcoma.

CAT scan/CT scan (computerized axial tomography)   A diagnostic test that uses X-rays and a computer to produce three-dimensional images of structures inside the body.

cell   The basic structural unit of all life.

central nervous system   The brain and spinal cord.

chromosome   A structure in the cell nucleus that carries genetic information in the form of genes.

clinical trial   A study to find out whether a new treatment is better or worse than existing treatments.

colony-stimulating factors (CSF)   Hormonelike substances that stimulate the production of blood cells. CSF treatments can help blood-forming tissue recover from the effects of chemotherapy and radiation therapy. Colony-stimulating factors include granulocyte colony-stimulating factors such as Neupogen and granulocyte/macrophage colony-stimulating factors.

complete blood count (CBC)   A sample of blood that counts red blood cells, white blood cells, and platelets.

cytokines   Proteins produced by immune system cells that affect the immune response, including histamine, prostaglandin, and interleukins. Cytokines can be detected in the lab with either an ELISA or ELISPOT test. Cytokines also can be produced in the laboratory and given to people to influence immune response.

cytopenia   A reduction in the number of various types of blood cells.

diuretic   A drug that increases the volume of urine. It acts by prompting the excretion of water and salts from the kidneys.

DNA   Deoxyribonucleic acid. One of two nucleic acids (the other is RNA) found in the nucleus of all cells. DNA contains genetic information that affects cell growth, division, and function.

enzyme   A protein that promotes essential functions involved in cell growth and metabolism.

eosinophils   A type of white blood cell that normally plays a role in the immune system; they may be higher in eosinophil leukemia.

extravasation   Inadvertent leakage of a chemotherapy drug out of the vein and into the skin.

genes   The basic unit of genetic material found in the nucleus of the cell. Genes contain hereditary information that is transferred from cell to cell.

hemoglobin   A protein in red blood cells that carries oxygen from the lungs to the body's tissues.

killer cell   A type of white blood cell that can kill tumor or germ cells.

leukemia   A type of carcinoma that affects the blood.

leukocyte   Another name for a white blood cell. *See* white blood cell.

lymph   A clear fluid, including white blood cells and a few red blood cells, through which cells travel as they fight disease.

lymphatic system   A network of vessels, tissue, and organs that produce and store cells that fight infection, along with the network of channels that carry lymph.

lymph gland   Also known as a lymph node, this bean-sized tissue contains white blood cells that filter the lymphatic fluid. Clusters of these glands are found under the arms and in the groin, neck, chest, and abdomen.

lymphocyte   Type of white blood cell that helps to produce antibodies and other substances that fight infection and diseases. Lymphocytes include B cells, which make antibodies that attack bacteria and toxins, and T cells, which attack body cells once they have been invaded by viruses or become malignant.

lymphoma   A type of cancer that originates in the lymphatic system and then affects the immune system.

macrophage   A type of white blood cell that is an important part of the immune system and is being studied as a possible type of biological therapy for cancer.

magnetic resonance imaging (MRI)   A nonradioactive scanning technique that uses magnetic waves to provide a cross-sectional image of structures inside the body.

mast cell   A type of white blood cell that doesn't circulate in the body, found primarily in the skin and gastrointestinal tract. Mast cells contain histamine and heparin, which are released during inflammation and during an allergic response.

metastasis   Cancer that has spread from the site of origin to another part of the body, usually through the lymphatic system or the blood.

monoclonal antibodies   A substance produced in the lab that can locate and bind to cancer cells wherever they are in the body. Many monoclonal antibodies are used in cancer diagnosis or treatment. Each one recognizes a different protein on certain cancer cells. Monoclonal antibodies can be used alone, or they can be used to deliver drugs, toxins, or radioactive material directly to a tumor.

myeloid   Derived from or pertaining to bone marrow.

neoadjuvant chemotherapy   Chemotherapy given before surgery in an attempt to shrink a malignant tumor.

neutrophil   A type of white blood cell that destroys and removes bacteria.

oncologist   Physician whose primary interest is cancer.

platelet   A type of blood cell that helps prevent bleeding by forming blood clots.

polyp   A growth that protrudes from a mucous membrane.

positron emission tomography (PET) scan   This imaging test uses computerized pictures of areas inside the body to find cancer cells. During this test, the patient is given an injection and a machine takes computerized pictures of areas inside the body.

protein   A molecule made up of amino acid chains that the body needs for proper function. Proteins form the structure of skin, hair, enzymes, cytokines, and antibodies.

protocol   A detailed treatment plan.

radiation sensitizer   Chemicals that make a cell more susceptible to the effects of radiation therapy.

radioisotope   An unstable element that releases radiation as it breaks down. Radioisotopes can be used in imaging tests or as a treatment for cancer.

red blood cell   A cell (also called an *erythrocyte*) that carries oxygen to all parts of the body and contains hemoglobin.

sarcoma   A type of cancer that originates in muscle cells and connective tissues; there are two broad groups: those that begin in the bone (bone cancer) and those that start from soft tissue (soft tissue sarcoma).

spinal tap   Also called a "lumbar puncture," this test collects a sample of the spinal fluid to be examined under a microscope. A needle is used to remove fluid from the spine in the lower back in a process that typically causes only mild, temporary discomfort.

stem cell   Cell from which other types of cells can develop.

T cell   A type of white blood cell that attacks invaders such as cancer cells and produces substances that regulate the immune response.

ultrasound   A diagnostic test that uses high-frequency sound waves to create images of organs and tissues inside the body. During this completely painless test, a technician moves a small device over an area on the patient's body, as an image appears on the computer screen.

white blood cell   A cell made by bone marrow to help the body fight infection and other diseases. White blood cells include lymphocytes, neutrophils, eosinophils, macrophages, and mast cells.

READ MORE ABOUT IT

APPEARANCE

Gafni, Ramy. *Ramy Gafni's Cancer Beauty Therapy: The Ultimate Guide to Looking and Feeling Great While Living with Cancer.* New York: M. Evans and Company, Inc., 2005.

Ovitz, Lori M. *Facing the Mirror with Cancer: A Guide to Using Makeup to Make a Difference.* London: Belle Press, 2004.

CANCER INFORMATION

Caldwell, Wilma R., ed. *Cancer Information for Teens: Health Tips About Cancer Awareness, Prevention, Diagnosis, and Treatment.* Teen Health Series. Detroit: Omnigraphics, 2004.

Carney, Karen L. *What Is Cancer Anyway?: Explaining Cancer to Children of All Ages.* Wethersfield, Conn.: Dragonfly Publishing, Inc., 1998.

Russell, Neil. *Can I Still Kiss You?: Answering Your Children's Questions About Cancer.* Deerfield Beach, Fla.: Health Communications Inc, 2001.

CANCER IN THE FAMILY

Babcock, Elise. *When Life Becomes Precious: The Essential Guide for Patients, Loved Ones, and Friends of Those Facing Serious Illnesses.* New York: Bantam, 1997.

Brown, Pamela. *Facing Cancer Together: How to Help Your Friend or Loved One.* Minneapolis: Augsburg Fortress Publishers, 1999.

Christ, Grace. *Healing Children's Grief: Surviving a Parent's Death from Cancer.* New York: Oxford University Press, 2000.

Heiney, Sue, Joan F. Hermann, Katherine V. Bruss, and Joy L. Fincannon. *Cancer in the Family.* Atlanta: American Cancer Society, 2001.

CHEMOTHERAPY AND RADIATION

Cukier, Daniel. *Coping with Chemotherapy and Radiation Therapy.* New York: McGraw-Hill, 2004.

Di Giacomo, Fran. *I'd Rather Do Chemo Than Clean Out the Garage: Choosing Laughter over Tears.* Dallas: Brown Books, 2003.

Lyss, Alan P. *Chemotherapy and Radiation for Dummies.* Hoboken, N.J.: Wiley, 2005.

McKay, Judith, and Nancee Hirano. *The Chemotherapy & Radiation Therapy Survival Guide.* Oakland, Calif.: New Harbinger Publications, 1998.

DIET AND NUTRITION

Chace, Daniella, and Maureen Keane. *What to Eat if You Have Cancer.* Updated 2nd ed. New York: McGraw-Hill, 2006.

——. *The What to Eat if You Have Cancer Cookbook.* New York: McGraw-Hill, 1997.

Dalzell, Kim. *Challenge Cancer and Win! Step-By-Step Nutrition Action Plans for Your Specific Cancer.* Round Lake, Ill.: Nutriquest Press, 2002.

Quillin, Patrick, and Noreen Quillin. *Beating Cancer with Nutrition.* Tulsa, Okla.: Nutrition Times Press, 2001.

FRIENDS WITH CANCER

Babcock, Elise. *When Life Becomes Precious: The Essential Guide for Patients, Loved Ones, and Friends of Those Facing Serious Illnesses.* New York: Bantam, 1997.

Brown, Pamela. *Facing Cancer Together: How to Help Your Friend or Loved One.* Minneapolis: Augsburg Fortress Publishers, 1999.

Fullbright, Colleen Dolan. *Cancer: How Friends Can Help.* New Brunswick, N.J.: Clear River Press, 2005.

Kalick, Rosanne. *Cancer Etiquette: What to Say, What to Do When Someone You Know or Love Has Cancer.* Oxford: Lion Books Publisher, 2005.

HEALTH TIPS FOR TEENS WITH CANCER

Caldwell, Wilma R. *Cancer Information for Teens: Health Tips about Cancer Awareness, Prevention, Diagnosis, and Treatment.* Detroit: Omnigraphics, 2004.

HOPE AND INSPIRATION

Girard, Vickie. *There's No Place Like Hope: A Guide to Beating Cancer in Mind-Sized Bites: A Book of Hope, Help, and Inspiration for Cancer*

Patients and Their Families. Seattle: Compendium Publishing & Communications, 2001.

HOW TO TALK ABOUT CANCER
Halpern, Susan P. *The Etiquette of Illness: What to Say When You Can't Find the Words.* London: Bloomsbury Publishing PLC, 2004.
Hope, Lori. *Help Me Live: 20 Things People with Cancer Want You to Know.* Berkeley, Calif.: Celestial Arts, 2005.

PARENTS WITH CANCER
Babcock, Elise. *When Life Becomes Precious: The Essential Guide for Patients, Loved Ones, and Friends of Those Facing Serious Illnesses.* New York: Bantam, 1997.
Brown, Pamela. *Facing Cancer Together: How to Help Your Friend or Loved One.* Minneapolis: Augsburg Fortress Publishers, 1999.
Christ, Grace. *Healing Children's Grief: Surviving a Parent's Death from Cancer.* New York: Oxford University Press, 2000.
Heiney, Sue, Joan F. Hermann, Katherine V. Bruss, and Joy L. Fincannon. *Cancer in the Family.* Atlanta: American Cancer Society, 2001.

TEENS WITH CANCER
Franzen, Carl. *The Other America—Teens with Cancer.* Chicago: Lucent Books, 2001.
Heiney, Sue, Joan F. Hermann, Katherine V. Bruss, and Joy L. Fincannon. *Cancer in the Family.* Atlanta: American Cancer Society, 2001.

INDEX